The Mayor
of
Seventeenth Avenue

a novel by

Tommie Lee

Also by Tommie Lee and available in paperback
or a variety of eBook formats:

Mulligan

For Four Players

NoThing

Chair de ma Chair

Mulligan's Daughters

These titles are available at *Smashwords*, the
Amazon Kindle store, *Barnes & Noble's NOOK* store,
and many online retailers.

Chair de ma Chair is available at *The Hammes
Notre Dame* bookstore.

- Find them all via tkcbooks.com -

First Print Edition
Published by Tommie Closson, Jr.
Distributed by CreateSpace

for Ryan Christopher Haukaas,

my dear friend, who should be here

1981 - 2012

The Mayor
of
Seventeenth Avenue

a novel, in which he is joined by...

a boy called Paper

a fair-hearted girl named Zoey

the ambitious Jimmy Nose

the angry Pete Gravy

an unfortunate young man called Dare

the devout and loyal Father Vaughan

a cat known as Chairman Meow

the Proud Prince

the kind-hearted Mr. Brandt

the misguided Mouse and Eddie

Erma, Buzzy, the Duck Man, the street people...

...and several unusual visitors

SEVENTEENTH AVE

Rain begins falling in the city on the first night of the incidents about 15 minutes before midnight.

A little dirty-haired blonde girl named Zoey sits at the bottom of the set of concrete steps that lead to her apartment. It is late, but it is also summer. She is only eight, but she is allowed to be outside until midnight *if* she stays in front of the building. She does. Most nights.

Other nights, she stays within a block of the brownstone and hides in the shadows, watching.

She tilts her face up to the heavens when she feels the first drops tap the top of her head. She squints and smiles as a few more of them begin to strike the steps around her. They make a rhythm, yes, but she hears more than that. The raindrops create a conversation of sorts that only she can understand.

Zoey pushes on her little knees and springs from the steps. Sang is just closing up the little Korean bodega next to her brownstone at Church and Seventeenth. Sang always keeps an eye on Zoey when she is out late. He was one of many who did so. Many children hang around in the neighborhood. Not all of them are fortunate enough to have a home, like Zoey does. All of the children, however, were friends. There is only *one* gang in this neighborhood, and they don't bother with Seventeenth much. No one does, really. For the most part, it's as forgotten as its homeless population.

Zoey holds out her arms. They are like a thin pair of pale wings. A smile spreads wide across her face that is equal parts mystery and mischief.

As the rain begins to fall a little harder, she is twirling. Twirling and dancing. Dancing and smiling. Smiling and savoring the moment.

Bradley Vincent drives up Church Street to the light and waits for his opportunity to turn left onto Seventeenth. As the rain finally becomes steady enough to make his wipers a good idea, he sees a little girl dancing in the rain on the side of the road.

He leans over to roll down his passenger side window and calls out to her. He is a third year medical student in the ER at St. Brigid Regional Hospital, and has yet to afford a car with electric windows.

The hospital is only three blocks from here. The staff at the hospital knows all of the regulars on the avenue.

"Zoey!" His voice is friendly, trusting.

"Doctor Brad!" Her reply is excited, exasperated.

He laughs and gives her a warm smile that she knows pretty well. "Go in the house before you catch a cold, kiddo!"

"Okay, Doctor Brad!"

Her arms fall down at her sides, as the air has been completely taken out of her little happy dance balloon. When she sighs at him, she sighs with her entire little body.

The sight of her full-body sigh makes Sang laugh as he clicks the lock on the shutters of his bodega. He gives Zoey's mother a wave. She has been standing in the kitchen, watching her daughter play. She waves back at Sang and smiles. Such a nice man that Sang.

The light turns green and Doctor Brad turns toward the hospital.

Zoey twirls a few times at the steps, and the rain begins to fall harder as she walks up them for the night.

She'll be back out before morning. Zoey is a very light sleeper. Her mother is not.

It has settled in nicely. There is a warm feeling of comfort, of clarity of purpose.

It has been away far too long. This time and this place feel like they were the right decisions.

This place is secure and comfortable, in the middle of a busy city that will afford great potential. The time has come to do as much work as can be done before the other side discovers it. It is only a question now of how much work that will be.

There is so much to do. It has been a very

long time since there has been time to come here and do this work. The hunger and desire are great.

This place is a perfect place to start.

This place is a perfect place to dispense the judgment.

This place is a perfect place to *feed...*

Soon, it is just after 4:30 in the morning in the city.

And cities, as they say, never sleep.

This is not particularly the case, though. Anyone who has ever attempted to buy alcohol in Portland after a certain hour, for example, gets the distinct impression that Fundamentalist Quakers whose descendants shut everything down at 10:30 p.m. settled it. Perhaps to go home and watch the Trailblazers lose again.

The exception, though, is the rule. Every now and then New York City has a blackout. When they come, parts of the city still find ways to stay awake. Even when the bulk of the citizens tend to avoid the darkened streets. This offers much credence for the theory of self-preservation.

Then again, there are sleepy parts of *some* cities that would hardly notice a power outage.

Other cities shake off the occasional hurricane because their citizens know that to live near the water means living *in it* every now and then. *It's cool, man. Sit back. Have a mojito. Check out that lightning.*

Cities have their own personality. In many

respects, they all appear to be the same, but they are not. If all one sees of cities are their airports they will never see the life they can have. In addition, if all they see of cities are the busy downtown areas they will never see how deeply they can sleep.

This city *sleeps*.

On the west side, where her streets begin to reach into the tree-rimmed mountains, it sleeps particularly soundly.

Erma Gird sleeps in early morning silence. There is almost nothing to hear in this part of the city at this hour. Even the ambulance bay of the nearby hospital is quiet. At this altitude, insect noise is always a non-factor in the deep of the night.

She sleeps between the two halves of a discarded cardboard refrigerator box behind an appliance store on the corner of Port and Seventeenth. It sits at the edge of the building that comprises half of Market Plaza, a strip mall of Mom & Pop stores desperately trying to stay afloat in the new economy and the era of the superstores.

Much of the business the strip mall sees comes from families who don't want to wander far from their loved ones at St. Brigid Regional Hospital, a block away. Because people at hospitals who are very worried about loved ones need to get *out* of the hospital for a while now and then. Some of them pop into the little restaurant called *Skillet* to try delicious and affordable local food. It is prepared by a talented woman named

Ruth who has never left the city and likely never will. Far more of these hospital visitors, however, go with what they know and eat at the Hacienda three doors down. Such is the new world.

Erma has an agreement with the owner of the appliance store. *Stay out of the way and make sure the traffic can't see you, and you can stay in back one night per week.* She has a similar deal with several merchants, up and down Seventeenth. She hates staying at the women's shelter two blocks over on Church Street. They make her take showers. She doesn't smell like herself after a shower. It is bad enough having to spend most of each winter there, never smelling like herself.

As with any city, there are a number of homeless citizens in the city. A small pocket of them has flocked to the area around Seventeenth Avenue on the periphery of the downtown district.

Seventeenth ends at the hospital, so to travel this far down, one has to have a reason. Traffic seeking to go west beyond St. Brigid will take Fifteenth or Nineteenth, both of which lead to the freeway system that runs alongside the mountains. Therefore, Seventeenth has the advantage of being somewhat quieter and less travelled. Except during morning and afternoon rush, when a great number of citizens think they are being clever and avoiding traffic by taking Seventeenth. In doing so, they ultimately create the very gridlock that they had sought to avoid in the first place. People are never so foolish than when they think they are being clever.

The lack of traffic makes it the perfect environment for the homeless to be comfortable, and out of the way. Society as a whole doesn't have to see them that often…and furthermore, the homeless are happy not to have to see much of society.

An old Ford LTD, a massive piece of machinery painted the color of cheap mustard, pulls into the Market Plaza merchant parking area. Ruth MacClaire parks in the space directly behind the back door of Skillet and turns off the engine, which shudders and sputters as it ceases all operations. The sound of the door creaking open is like a tomb in a Lugosi movie. When it slams shut, the sound is like Thor's hammer slamming into Captain America's shield.

Getting out of the car with a loud thump, Ruth spots Erma and bids her good morning with a smile.

"Good morning, Erma," Ruth says.

Ruth has only really been half-asleep. A '79 LTD makes for one hell of an alarm clock once it reaches a certain age.

Erma likes Ruth. If she promises to sleep behind the restaurant or the appliance store no more than once per week, Ruth will make her some breakfast and give her extra toast that she can keep in her pockets.

Later, Erma gives a triangle of toast to her friend who lives farther along the avenue. He is known as The Mayor, and he presides over the melting pot of the forgotten that is Seventeenth Avenue. It is its own city within the city.

***

In the middle of the afternoon, Erma doubles back to Market Plaza after a lunch at the soup kitchen up on Twentieth Avenue. She's in the parking area behind Hacienda when she spots Jimmy Nose coming out of the drugstore in the opposite building with his Dramamine.

Erma likes Jimmy. She has fond memories of his late mother, a close friend of hers when they were school girls.

Jimmy likes Erma. She has a wagging tongue when it comes to valuable information he may be able to work to his advantage. Additionally, she never asks for much in return. She also has great stories about his mom, on those rare occasions when he wants to sit and listen to them.

Both Jimmy and Erma view each other the same: Not the most pleasant person to be around, but there's an underlying loyalty at work that keeps them invested in making sure the other is getting by okay. Mostly because they give each other things.

"What's the latest, Erma?" Jimmy stays downwind as he asks this. She's looking particularly grubby today…no easy feat on a rainy day like this, and yet she manages to pull it off with verve.

Erma walks over to Jimmy, looks at the parking lot, and smiles.

"Hi, Jimmy. I heard a good one last night."

Jimmy leans up against his Ford Bronco and

drops the pharmacy bag in through the open window. The rain has been taking a break for a few hours now, and many people are enjoying the chance to rest their AC. He sets the keys on the roof and puts his hands in his jeans pockets.

"I hear there's a treasure at St. George's. Somethin' *real* special. An' no one knows it's even there. Maybe not even Father Vaughan."

Jimmy leans forward. "Go on."

"I ain't sure what it is," Erma mumbles. "But I heard it from Sophie. Sophie's sister is married to an art museum guy. They met Father Vaughan to talk about their daughter's wedding, and he saw the treasure. Told Sophie later on that it was a very special piece. An artifact."

She pauses, distracted by something, before continuing. "Sophie didn't say what it was, though."

"An artifact. That's…that's *it*? That's all ya got?"

The old woman's first reply to the question is a thick, bronchial cough. One built up by years of smoking coupled with living in the cold street and the thin mountain air.

"I wouldn' lie to ya, Jimmy. I know better. Besides, we go back too far. I got nothin' to gain from hidin' anything."

"Fair enough, Erma."

Jimmy Nose is a small-time criminal, but he runs with a family from the South side. Being part of a crew means having everyone else afraid of you. Well, everyone but The Mayor. And everyone in The Family thinks that old man is just crazy anyway.

It also means the only way to move up was to earn. To earn well involves finding creative ways to find revenue. Paying the proper tributes above you. Building reputation and respect. This isn't as easy as it sounds.

There is a delicate balance involved in finding the subtle ways to rip off the people in your neighborhood without losing face with them. For the most part, Jimmy Nose mastered this balance years ago. This, though, is something else. This has the potential to be something pretty big. Assuming it's true.

"This is ripping off a..." he pauses, looks around, and lowers his voice before finishing his sentence... "a *church*, Glenda. The church I was baptized in, took communion in." *Got my first hand-job in,* he doesn't add. After all, she knew his mother, God rest her soul.

"You asked me what I heard, Jimmy. That's what I heard. So what ya GOT for me?"

Jimmy smiles, and reaches into the pocket of his well-oiled black leather coat. He pulls out a pack of cigarettes with a book of matches stuck in the plastic wrapping. He shakes the pack and pulls two of them out with the corner of his mouth. He lights them with a match, and hands one to the old woman. She accepts it like a child being handed a chocolate Easter Bunny.

He stuffs the matchbook back into the plastic and reaches into his pants-pocket. His fingers emerge with a ten-dollar bill, which he hands to her.

She accepts the bill with a smile in a cloud of smoke. Jimmy begins to put the cigarettes back in his coat, and tosses her the pack instead.

"Thanks, Jimmy."

"As usual, we didn't talk, right?"

"Right."

"If your lead pans out, I'll give ya another twenty."

"Thanks, Jimmy," she says, but by this point he is already shutting the door of his Bronco and rolling up the window. A rumble of thunder in the mountains suggests this is a good idea.

Erma looks up at the clouds rolling down the side of the nearest peak. The way storms literally roll down the side of the mountains is something that cannot be described, it has to be seen.

She wanders off to find shelter.

Jimmy Nose nurses the starter on the old truck, and it rumbles awake.

An artifact at St. George's. Something valuable, but not particularly memorable or noticeable. Something that might perhaps be easy to fence over the state line before anyone really knew it was gone and not all that traceable after that.

Too good to be true.

Jimmy Nose waits to turn left onto Seventeenth and looks to his right. Up the street in the direction of St. George's, he waits for his turn to pull out. The church is down there, but it is hard to see from this angle thanks to the 30 floors of the Porter Building directly across the street from it.

The street will be completely quiet tonight, maybe eight or nine hours from now. Time enough to run home, get some sleep, grab his tools, and have a few more drinks to steel his reserve.

For the first time in the past year, he is glad his mother isn't alive to see the day her son would break into her church.

Times change. The game didn't. If he is going to win a hand or two in the game of life…James Michael Nosetti has to up the *sin ante* a bit every now and then.

The room is quiet as a tomb. He can hear nothing but his breathing, his own heartbeat. He barely registers any sound at all from the one who addresses him until the first word is spoken. The voice is powerful and vast, a voice that feels as if it might be capable of tearing down the walls of an ancient city on the Mediterranean.

HEAR ME, MY SON. FOR YOU ARE A DEVOTED SERVANT OF THE LORD OUR GOD. REJOICE, FOR THIS GREAT GIFT HAS BEEN BESTOWED UPON YOU WITH GREAT INTENT AND PURPOSE BY THE LORD OUR GOD.

"Forever in His glory, bathed in the light of His love. Amen. Thank you, Blessed One, for showing me a higher calling."

ARE YOU PREPARED IN YOUR HEART TO DO WHAT MUST BE DONE?

"I am," he whispers, fighting back the tears.

ARE YOU PREPARED TO DO THE LORD'S WORK AND FILL HIS DIVINE PURPOSE?

"I am," he repeats. He continues to kneel, but looks up into the face of the one who has shown him a new way to serve his God. The one who has brought a freshness to his faith. The one who has come into his life so suddenly, and helped define the central purpose for it. The one who has brought a new energy to his life.

"I am an instrument of The Lord Our God. You are His vessel. With your guidance to shore me up, my courage will sustain me to the great work that lies before me."

The temperature in this place, already a little cool to begin with, drops suddenly. The afternoon sun is absent, as rain laps against the walls of his church.

GO TO YOUR HOME THEN, MY SON. REST YOURSELF AND PREPARE TO SERVE GOD WITH YOUR ENTIRE HEART.

"As I begin each day, it shall be," he says. "And as each day should end."

Two in the morning. Wednesday has been wet so far, as was Tuesday. The street is as quiet as he knew it would be. He's been keeping a watchful eye for the last 10 minutes and hasn't even seen a single car.

He parks his Bronco between the narrow white lines behind Sully's Music Store on Nineteenth and Church. Old man Sully hasn't repainted his lot since the mini-car craze of the 70s, and parking there is always a pain in the ass if you don't drive a sedan or something smaller. He locks it and walks the two blocks to the St. George's Catholic Church.

Jimmy clings to the shadows to stay out of the line-of-sight of the traffic cameras. He makes his way to the basement stairwell to pick whatever lock is there on the door and get himself into the building.

Thirty minutes later, he surrenders. The lock is the most formidable opponent he has ever encountered in two decades with a lock pick. He pulls the collar of his coat up and goes around to the front of the building.

There is a rumble of thunder, and he can hear one of the cats in Adrian's Alley in the relative silence as it jumps off a garbage can and sends the lid clattering to the ground.

He really has no choice but to go through the front door. The side doors will only lead to more locks. He knows this because he knows this church very well.

He hides in the shadows for a few minutes, studying the traffic camera on the light pole. He is counting, getting a feel for how long he'll have to pick the lock and get into the church before he's recorded in the process.

The moment the pivoting camera swings away from the front entrance of St. George's Catholic Church, Jimmy emerges from the darkness and sweeps up to the ornate doors.

3...4...5...6...

His fingers are flying around his tools as he works the mechanism with everything he has. He is listening so intently for the tumblers that if a spider on the other side of the door passed gas…he would hear it.

11…12…13…

Halfway point. Time to focus. Time to push through this and…get the lock…to just…

22…23…not going to make it…Plan B…

He grabs the maul hammer from his bag and smacks the fat end of the lock. It breaks, and he pushes the heavy door with everything he's worth.

As he slips in and pushes the door shut, his internal stopwatch hits *30.*

The camera records the closing of the door, but nothing else.

He exhales and looks around in the darkness of the entry hall. His heartbeat is elevated a bit, and he realizes part of him expected to find the ghost of his mother standing at the entrance of the chapel; arms crossed, tears of disappointment rolling down her wrinkled cheeks. For a moment, he can see her there.

He shakes off the visual and flips open his cell phone to use as a light to make sure he doesn't trip over anything on his way to the clergy stairs. Any item matching the description he was given would be locked in Father Vaughan's office.

When he reaches the stairs, he hesitates.

What sounds like a long, deep breath of air comes from the right-side hallway. The backlight on his phone goes out, and he flips it shut rather than press a button to bring it back. He won't need it here. He knows this hallway well. Like most of the kids he grew up with, Jimmy Nosetti walked this hall in single-file on his way to Sunday School. This hallway is full of memories. Now he's creating one of a different sort

He passes by the open door of one of the pre-school classrooms, and once again sees his mother's ghost glaring at him. Her arms crossed, the tears flowing.

He blinks, and she's gone again.

"Sorry, ma."

YOUR MOTHER IS NOT GOING TO ANSWER YOU, JAMES.

The voice is deep and powerful, filling the hall and nearly filling his tighty-whities at the same time. At the very least, he's sure he wet himself a tiny bit.

He reaches into his waistband and pulls out a small handgun.

"Who's there?" His question hangs in the darkness like a line of wet laundry, slowly rolling out toward the doorway to the basement.

There is no reply.

He stands perfectly still, the thin scent of ammonia wafting up from his crotch. Another draw of wind from down the hall comes, and then another. They seem to be coming from the cellar.

He takes a single, perfectly silent step in the direction of the air-sucking noise.

HAVE YOU COME TO CONFESS YOUR SINS, MY CHILD?

"Father?"

COME TO ME, AND I WILL SHOW YOU THE PATH TO THE REWARD YOU SEEK.

He snaps the gun, loading a round in the chamber, and continues to move to the basement stairs.

COME, MY CHILD.

Everything in Jimmy Nose says to turn around and run out of the church. Everything that is but his feet, which continue to move toward the stairs.

By the time he reaches the top of the stairs, calmness has overwhelmed his senses. By the time he gingerly places a foot on the first step, he no longer even has the gun in his hand. A peaceful state of mind has moved over him, and it is without fear that he walks down the old wooden stairs, closing the door behind him.

The Mayor of Seventeenth Avenue wakes early. He does so almost every day of the week. He enjoys watching the sun come up through the skyscrapers on his avenue. Soon the sun will pull itself up into the August sky and try to be noticed through the thin layer of purple rain clouds that seems to have a firm grip on the city these days.

The city has plenty of authority figures. It boasts one of the most efficient police departments in the American west. The City Commissioners and the Mayor's Office work together with the kind of united efficiency most of the other major cities in America can only dream of. Being a large city, there is an element of organized crime. This is inevitable. However, for the most part, they stay out of the way here on Seventeenth. It has been this way for some time now in this part of the downtown district.

Here on the far west side it is pretty much understood that The Mayor of Seventeenth Avenue is just that. The city government and the municipal police stay out of his way, and he promises to stay out of theirs. He works with them, they work with him, and the job gets done.

Seventeenth, it should be noted, has a fairly sizeable homeless population.

The thoroughfare is tucked out of the way, has only a couple of the city's skyscrapers on it, and ends at the huge hospital known as St. Brigid Regional. Seventeenth's solitude attracts the forgotten, the quiet, the people of specific purpose who are unlikely to give things much of a second look. The opposite end of Seventeenth, on the East Side, is the arts district. Far more populated, far more popular. Here, it is quiet.

Everyone looks up to the man called The Mayor, and understands that what he says goes.

The Mayor of Seventeenth Avenue is uniquely attuned to the homeless on his part of the Avenue. Most likely because he is one of them.

He always rises early, but this morning he woke up even more so. He has been rousted from his sleep by bad dreams. This has happened a lot lately and never used to. The Mayor has been fighting with dragons in the hours before he awakens. He isn't sure how dragons fit into anything.

The Mayor walks around his cellar a bit and straightens things up. He likes to keep his area clean each day before he heads out to watch the sun rise. It's a beautiful sight from here this time of year, framed by the twin HCR Towers on Eighteenth and Tel Comm Tower on Sixteenth. Mr. Brandt, the building manager, is kind enough to allow The Mayor to live in the Pierce building. The Mayor likes to think that keeping the place nice is part of his end of the bargain.

He emerges from the bottom stairwell of the Pierce building, 40 floors high itself and the tallest building on either end of Seventeenth Avenue. As he does so he is spotted by a police car sitting at the stoplight at Grove Street, waiting to cross Seventeenth.

"Who's the homeless guy?" asks the rookie in the passenger seat. His crisp new uniform already has a fresh jelly stain on it from this morning's breakfast. This is his second day on the job, and his first on the road with Sgt. Zachary.

"That's The Mayor."

The rookie looks at his sergeant with that special look of confusion that only a true neophyte can pull off.

"The Mayor of Seventeenth Avenue. He's kind of...he's...he's like the mayor here."

"He has his own part of the city?"

"Not officially, of course. He just...*runs* things here."

"*He* runs things? Not the West Side Kings? Or Pete Gravy's crew?"

"No. he actually keeps them in check. He's not a criminal. He's something of a…guardian angel for the street."

"And we can trust him?"

"We have for years."

The rookie takes a sip of some kind of pretentious overpriced coffee. He manages to do so without adding a new stain to his uniform. "So where did he come from? How long has he been here?"

"No one's really sure how he came here, how he suddenly became the final word on the street, or even when. He was off the radar for a while before we knew about him, which I guess was about eight years ago. See, The Mayor is a perfect example of 'the right person in the right place at the right time. He's got that whatchacallit…that *charisma.* He's the kind of guy that can motivate people to do the right thing when they don't wanna. He pushes the people around here to go beyond their usual capacity to do good things. He gets the people around here to watch out for each another in situations where you would expect it to be 'every man for himself'."

"I see."

"More importantly, kid, he commands respect. I think it's because he can pull things to his advantage in tough situations."

"How do you mean?"

"The Mayor's a motivator. He's a Field General. He's a coach and he's a head cheerleader."

"It sounds like you have a lot of respect for

him."

"Most of us do. The smart ones, anyway. And if you wanna last on this beat...you will too. Next time we're down this way, I'll introduce you. Just always remember one thing about The Mayor."

"What's that?"

The sergeant grinned, noticing for the first time that the light had changed some time ago. No one was behind them at this hour anyway, so he made his turn without comment or care.

"Remember that The Mayor has the uncanny ability to call in favors. Favors with us, favors with the people under his "protection", favors with the mob, even favors with the Kings."

The car rolls on toward the hospital, in the opposite direction of The Mayor.

There is another mystery, every bit equal to the story surrounding The Mayor's arrival to this part of the city. No one is quite certain how he has kept the level of crime on his street so low, as he is hardly a fearful feature of it. Given the lack of intimidation he presents, it is entirely possible that he wonders the same thing. Somehow, though, people respect the street and leave it alone. Likewise, The Mayor has held onto a thin but formidable level of respect and reverence, and has enjoyed very little trouble from any part of the city's criminal element.

The street is calm and quiet, as it always is. A police car had lingered at the light for a moment. The Mayor hadn't noticed who was driving, thanks to the thin streetlight and the tinted windshield, but if he had to hazard a guess, it was probably Sergeant Zachary. The Mayor likes Sergeant Zachary. He knows a bent cop when he sees one, and that man is as honest as the day is long.

He crosses Grove Street and spots a couple of the early workout enthusiasts strolling into Contours. They both wear leotards that seem far too fancy and expensive to do much sweating in, and they carry designer bags that cost enough to feed most of The Mayor's friends for a month. The secret love of his life is not among them.

He walks on. In the alley behind the 17-floor Adrian Hotel, which everyone in the neighborhood refers to as Adrian's Alley, The Mayor sees a burn-barrel in use.

A long-haired burnout named Buzzy is standing at it, warming away the last of the overnight chill. Even in summer, the air is cold at night. This is how life is when you live outdoors in a city located this high in the mountains.

"Mornin' Mayor."

"Buzzy."

The Mayor walks over and warms his hands a bit. "Supposed to rain again today. Wettest stretch of August in a number of years, they say."

Buzzy is distracted. "I guess."

The Mayor smiles. "It probably makes you think of home, doesn't it? What's the old song? 'It never rains in Southern California'?"

"Mmmm," Buzzy says. It is a syllable devoid of emotion.

The fire in the barrel crackles, and it smells of

green wood. The Mayor correctly assumes a shipping palate has been broken up for it.

"Something troubling you, Buzzy?"

Buzzy shrugs.

"I assure you, our unpleasant business is behind us. Your debt to me is fulfilled."

Buzzy nods. "I know."

The Mayor presses because that's what he does. "Truly, Buzzy...is there anything I can help with?"

Buzzy claps his hands together. Staring into the fire has given him a bit of focus. In a mind usually rife with flashbacks from Haight-Ashbury and a summer of love so very long ago, moments of focus are rare.

"Nah. I'm good. Have a good day, Mr. Mayor."

"Stay clean, Buzzy. Do not forget that you owe this community a great debt from the last time you slipped away into old habits."

Buzzy says nothing, and walks up the alley toward Eighteenth Avenue. Ahead of him, cars are beginning to roll down Eighteenth toward Church Street. Most of them are doing 35 miles per hour in a 30 mile per hour zone, as usual.

The large cat called Chairman Meow watches Buzzy walk by, happy to have the man out of his alley again. Buzzy unnerves him, mostly because of his unusual and unpleasant smells.

The cat leaps off a large hard rubber trash barrel and lands with a thud on the blacktop. He carries considerable bulk, and his movement is fluid and graceful...formidable.

He strolls casually up to The Mayor and walks a figure-eight between the man's feet, dragging his tail around his ankles like a fuzzy python.

"Good boy, Chairman." He reaches down and pats the yellow-eyed devil on the top of the head. Very few in the world are granted this privilege by Chairman Meow. The Mayor is one of them, for reasons only The Chairman remembers.

The sounds of morning are building the crescendo of their symphony. The city is waking up for another day.

Some hours later, the lunch crowd has begun to file in and out of Pete's Zeria.

Pete's Zeria sits at the corner of Sixteenth Avenue and Church Street. It has no affiliation whatsoever with Pete's Party Store and Hoagie Shop, which sits by the tracks at Seventeenth and Sawyer serving entirely different food made by an entirely different Pete. Both Petes played football at Western High together and come from established Italian families.

Pete of Pete's Zeria is known as Pete Gravy, because his red sauce is the life's blood of the community. There's a flavor in his spaghetti and pizza sauce that is unmatchable.

The neon sign above his entrance is usually considered to be clever. It reads *Pizzeria* one way, and then when the neon moves it crosses out the *Piz* at the beginning and scribbles *Pete's* above it with an arrow pointing at the lined-out letters.

At the moment, however; the second Z is not working, and so it says *Pete's eria* when the second lights are lit. In this configuration, though, it still accomplishes what he wanted, and it's cheaper than getting it fixed. It's still clever enough to make Pete's customers smile.

Unlike his sign's errant consonant, Pete Gravy is…connected.

His father was a hell of a chef, and taught him everything he knows. About everything. About how to cook. About how to show your wife the back of your hand every once in a while. About how to be a part of the criminal element in this community without attracting too much attention to yourself.

His old man was never more than a bit of muscle for the real power, though. He never rose to the level his son has. Pete runs his own crew, and he treats his crew very well. Like he treats his customers. Like he treats his kids. Like he treats pretty much everyone but his wife…and his girlfriend.

Mouse and Eddie are at one of the red and white table-clothed tables near the window that looks across the street at Tel Comm Tower. It's 60 stories high and casts a hell of an afternoon shadow on the place. Eddie is having a slice with anchovies. Mouse is dumping what looks like a pound of grated cheese that smells like dirty feet onto a basket of spaghetti with sausage in it. The fennel seeds in the sausage are at just the right temperature to secrete the spicy flavor that reminds him of his Nana's recipe.

Mouse loves it here. Eddie thinks the sausage is a little weak.

"Jimmy did it on spec. Don't be mad at him, Pete," Eddie says. But Eddie isn't connected, and he doesn't understand how these things work.

Eddie and Mouse aren't a part of "the family". They do, however, understand it all too well. They all grew up in the same neighborhood together. They've known Pete and Jimmy since they were all wetting themselves in daycare.

Mouse says nothing, twirling his fork in the basket of pasta. He wraps a good quarter of an inch of noodles around the fork and then stabs a piece of sausage. He envies his mouth at this moment.

"So where is he?"

Mouse and Eddie look at him, wide-eyed. Pete said that a little louder than most people would have. Five tables of customers are pretending nothing is going on at the window table right now. The regulars at Pete's Zeria are very accustomed to doing that. Most of them are from the neighborhood. The majority of the transplants who work in the skyscrapers don't eat here, except for the Tel Comm people across the street who enjoy the convenience.

"Nobody knows, Pete," says Eddie. Mouse shrugs with his mouth full, trying not to chew in any sudden movements. He sits still as if he were the one Pete were mad at, as if Pete was a T-Rex and his vision was based on movement.

"Jimmy shouldn't tackle something like this

on his own. If he pulled it off and decided to pull a vanishing act..."

Eddie raises his eyebrows as he cuts him off.

"I'm gonna stop ya there, Pete. You're surrounded by civilians. Present company included."

Mouse nods and swallows a piece of sausage.

Pete Gravy notices that the conversation in his place picked back up suddenly, which means he hadn't realized it had waned at all.

Without a word, he wipes the tablecloth with a rag that smells like old dishwater, and disappears back into the kitchen.

Pete is part of the same crew as Jimmy, a rung above him on the ladder, more than a little miffed that Jimmy took it upon himself to tackle something of this size alone. Trying to hog the spotlight and cut Pete out of any tributes. It's hard enough scratching out a living in this neighborhood. The head of the family has a soft spot for The Mayor. Pete doesn't need one of the people he depends on for his living trying to pass him by.

Jimmy needs to either show up soon and explain himself...or just keep running to wherever he's bolted to. Because Heaven help him if he surfaces now without a good excuse.

In the meantime...Pete Gravy has work to do.

He wants to find out more about what was so damned important at St. George's.

***

Paper doesn't understand the note.

"So, 'Nose in sg 250 no out' means *what*, exactly?"

Zoey has to explain a lot of her notes. She isn't particularly good at the note part of her job as one of Paper's street spies. She makes up for it by being very, very good at the Not Sleeping Much, Sneaking Out At All Hours, and Being Really Nosy parts of it.

She's sitting on the steps of her building, eating a cherry popsicle. Her mouth is rimmed with red from it, making her look a bit like the beloved clown from Channel Nine.

"Jimmy Nose went into St. George's at 2:50 this morning, Paper, an' he did'n come out."

Anyone else would have followed this with "That you *saw*." Paper doesn't say this, though. Paper knows just how tenacious Zoey is when it comes to her watching. If she says Jimmy didn't come back out, Jimmy didn't come back out.

What he *does* say, is, "So? Sanctuary, maybe? Sleepin' one off in the pews? Father Clifton used to let people…"

"Paper!" She looks like his mother does when she shouts his name. For a second, he can feel his spine wag a little bit. "Everybody knows he was lookin' for the treasure!"

"Okay. Go nose around in the church after your Ma makes you lunch. Stay around your block so you don't get grounded. You're my eyes on the church in case something fishy's going on. 'Kay?"

"'Kay," she smiles. "I'm your eyes on the

church, Paper."

Paper gives her a kiss on the forehead. She blushes because she loves him, in that special way that only little girls can love someone other than family.

Paper heaves a heavy sigh and rubs the stump where his right hand used to be. He stops to stifle a cough.

The Mayor needs to know about this.

"It has already arrived at St. George's Catholic Church. It has already begun to gather strength."

The room is filled with bright light as the two figures walk slowly around it, actually circling the room absent-mindedly. Both of them are dressed in immaculate suits: one blue, one black. The flare of the light would have made it difficult for anyone else to make out their features, but the two of them know each other well. *Very* well. Oddly enough, they also seem to be giving off their own light. One blue, and one…darker, almost black.

"Father Vaughan," the figure in blue replies, gliding across the floor effortlessly. "He is weak of will."

"Weak, yes. Weak by *design*. He has been warmed by the Glory since his journey to Rome."

"Is Vaughan aware of this?"

"He is not. It blinds him from the reality and from much of his own soul. However, it has failed to undo his heart. His heart will rise, and that will bear scrutiny."

"Vaughan will be sympathetic to the cause. He will…"

The figure in black interrupts the figure in blue. "Vaughan will do what his heart leads him to do, whether for our cause or the other. In this, he has strength. A strength with which we fail to credit him."

"And what of the Knight?"

The figure in the black suit stops circling, and fixes his gaze across the room at the figure in blue.

The light burns brighter still, a flare of white rimmed with yellow and indigo. The curtains and windows are all closed tight, and there is no additional light source in the room. It is dark outside, long into the night.

"I do not believe the city has yet been graced by the Knight. I fear that at least one or two brazen souls will rise to claim the role without having the heart for it."

Silence spreads out between them, broken by the whispering of a phantom breeze that could not exist in a room closed off from the rest of the world. It was not the whistle of a wind carrying rain, heard through a wall. It was more like the distant voices of the distressed and helpless at the bottom of a Jovian canyon.

The figure in blue smiles a crooked smile and speaks in a booming sound that is almost metallic in its timbre. "Perhaps a Knight will rise."

"Perhaps."

"You are not thinking of doing this yourself, are you? The mortal form suits your mind ill."

The figure in black says nothing. He doesn't have to. The two of them know all too well how he feels about this.

Rain begins to fall on the city again. It had not been forecasted to return until the middle of the week, a day or two from now.

It is going to rain a lot in the coming weeks, and the events are only just beginning to take root.

"You, of course, will remain."

The figure in the blue suit nods at his friend. "I will. It has been decreed from on high that I have some role to play yet."

"And yet you criticize me for considering taking an active hand in what is to unfold?"

"I said nothing of the sort," the figure in blue replies. "I merely asked if you were thinking about it. Reminding you of the usual result, and how..."

The figure in black takes a deep breath, which causes the other to pause. His voice is like a hammer when it speaks. "Let me delay you no further in learning what your role might be."

They share a smile. It is a sad smile, somehow, but there is genuine respect behind each of them.

"I wish you well and bid you tidings, brother."

"And I you," the figure in blue replies. The figure in black has already vanished, though. The light in the room has diminished sharply, and slowly burns itself out into nothing.

***

The Proud Prince walks out of the Pierce Building and finds his favorite bench facing it from Grove Park, across Seventeenth Avenue.

He opens the Velcro on the top of a nylon lunch bag and pulls out a sandwich, a bottle of ginger ale, and a sealable baggie of Funyuns.

He flips open a weathered copy of one of the Mickey Spillane books he never made time for in his younger days. He is about halfway through, and realizes why he never made time for it before.

"Grim reading face again today, Proud Prince?"

The Mayor is approaching him from the sidewalk, but keeping a bit of distance. The Mayor knows he doesn't always smell very good, and he can see the man is still eating. The Mayor is nothing if not observant and thoughtful. He gets close enough to read the cover.

"Killer Mine. Any good?"

Nicholas Prince takes a drink in order to clear his mouth before answering. "Not particularly, Mayor. But he's a classic author, and it's on my 'haven't read-it' list, and I found it at Spines for 25 cents.

"Exceptional deal, then."

"I suppose. It has disappointed so far. How are you coming with the Cormac McCarthy?"

"I've only just started it. I've been busy." The Mayor rubs the back of his head. "I leave you in peace, sir. Enjoy your lunch, enjoy your book. I am distracting you from both."

Prince smiles. "I enjoy our talks, my friend."

"You are a good man, Proud Prince. But I

have rounds to make."

The Proud Prince feels his phone vibrate. The Mayor takes that as his cue, and gestures farewell by touching his forehead and dropping his arm.

Nicholas Prince holds up a finger. The Mayor pauses.

Prince presses a button and banishes the call to his voicemail. "I wanted to talk to you about something strange."

"Certainly. At your service, good sir."

Prince puts his remaining food back in his bag, and leans forward on the bench. The Mayor takes the hint and leans in a bit.

"What do you know about...snakes?"

The Mayor pondered this for a moment. "Very little, I admit. Why?"

"Because I've seen three of them in the last two days, right here on Seventeenth."

The Mayor tightens his face in thought. "That's a bit...unusual."

"I thought so. I thought you might have some idea why."

"Here at the park?"

"Two of them, yes. One was at Church Street, though, yesterday."

The Mayor steps back. He suddenly has the urge to walk all around the park, staring at the path as he does so. He may not remember much of anything of the life he used to lead before he came here, but he's pretty sure he didn't like snakes very much in that life, either.

"I shall look into it. Thank you, Proud Prince."

With a wave, the man in the fancy suit smiles and picks himself up from the bench. A raindrop greets his face, and by the time he's back across the street and heading into the building…fat drops are slapping the sidewalk.

Father Vaughan listens to the rain as it starts to tickle his office windows. He pops the metal cap off the top of an ice cold glass bottle of Coke. Father Vaughan refuses to drink it from a plastic bottle. He grew up with the glass bottles. He drank it out of glass bottles at the seminary. The old familiar green friends were even there for him when he did his missionary work in the stifling jungles of Ecuador…even if they were usually lukewarm, at best.

His office is a shrine of Coca-Cola memorabilia. Polar Bears, Santa Clauses, tons of pieces from several countries in several languages.

He has a standing order with the local distributor for the small glass bottles. Only one of the machines in the part of the city even uses them any more. Father Vaughan used to keep a vintage bottle machine in his office stocked with them, but the motor in the damn thing gave out about six months ago, and he has yet to find the man who can repair it.

He also keeps a couple of cases of the bottles in his basement at home at all times, just like his parents did when he was growing up. They stay nice and cool down there. Here at the office, they live in a nice mini-fridge with a shelf that is the perfect height for them. Between work and home, he drinks about four a day. This is down from six, which was his daily intake for years and years until his doctor pointed out what a bad idea this was.

Additionally, as you might imagine, Father Vaughan does not have the nicest teeth in the world.

He glances at the clock. He has an hour. The planner on his desk is open with his favorite gel pen sitting in the median. Under Wednesday is written *Pre-Marital Counseling* with the first names of a nice young couple from the East Side. They'll be the sixteenth couple he has married, but only his fifth at St. George's. It has been an off year for weddings.

Below that are the words *Scout Overnight 7p.*

The mail sits on his desk, and grabs his letter opener to tuck into the envelopes. Boy Scout Troop business makes up most of it, as this is their busy season and the Church has always been a big supporter of the Troop.

From the basement, he is sure he can hear the breathing of his sleeping tenant.

He's suddenly concerned that it isn't just in his head. He takes another sip from the bottle and sets it down on a Coca-Cola coaster with a cork bottom. He walks briskly over to the vent.

He slaps it shut with his shoe, and the noise ceases.

The room is quiet enough to hear the air conditioning in the window of the room next door, and to hear the carbonation fizzing in his bottle of Coke.

Pete Gravy is very pissed-off.

"I'm very pissed off."

Pete is sitting at Honey's, at his usual barstool. Most people know to avoid that barstool, actually. Amy, the bartender he is seeing on the side is cleaning glasses and talking to her boss at the other end of the bar. Pete is tipping back single-malt with Tommy McMahon, a Capo from the north side, with whom he went to high school. If there is anyone he can trust in the upper management...it would be Tommy.

"Nose works for *me*. He knows this. He's supposed to understand the pecking order."

"The pecking order," Tommy agrees. There has been a lot of single malt up to this point, so they are talking a little heavily...and a little too loudly.

"This organization lives by the pecking order. It's the only reason it does, right?"

"Right," Tommy concurs.

"We don't rob who we ain't supposed to rob. We always kick upstairs. We keep The Mayor and his people out of it. And we *do not keep secrets from the people above us.*"

"Preachin' to the choir."

Pete Gravy is rolling now, and he drains his glass and holds it up in the direction of his girlfriend. Amy pulls a bottle of Glenmorangie down and saunters over to them.

"Thanks, babe," he says as she tops off the glass. She smiles at him. Smiling...and a few other things...keeps her in jewelry and keeps the landlord off her back. She's not used to saying much, but she gives him a look that hopefully expresses that he's talking a little too loudly about his business.

Pete Gravy misses the look entirely, as does his friend Tommy.

"Ripping off the church ain't the smartest idea, granted." Tommy says. "But these things become necessary sometimes. They just have to go through the proper channels."

"Exactly," Pete growls, swallowing his scotch. "You sit down, you have a conversation. Initiative is one thing, but stupidity will get you killed."

"Jimmy is being stupid," says Tommy, draining his Jack & Coke. "Amy?"

Amy nods in his direction.

"Jimmy is now guilty of two stupidities," Pete says, creating new words in the fine tradition of scotch drinkers throughout the ages. "He went freelance on the biggest church on the west side. And then he disappeared without checking in anywhere. He doesn't answer his phone, either."

Tommy shakes his head. Pete takes it a step further.

"If Jimmy Nose isn't dead, he's going to wish he was."

Amy takes Tommy's glass, and leans over to kiss Pete on the ear. As she does so, she whispers something in it.

"Jimmy? You know people are hearing you talk, right?"

He kisses her cheek and says nothing.

Before running into Tommy here at Honey's, Pete Gravy has just come from reporting to Ronnie Soak, the Polish Capo directly above him. The Mob in the city is diverse. Polish, Irish, Italian, Mexican, and Argentine...the whole of the Catholic Church is represented. They work together as well as any mob ever has.

Pete told Mikey about what had happened within his crew, and the decision was made that Pete needs to go into the church tomorrow night to figure out what's what. It can't be tonight, which is another reason why he's pissed.

Tonight is out because the Church is busy with a Boy Scout Overnight Campout thing. Pete Gravy fails to understand how it can be considered a campout if it's indoors. Maybe there are special rules for inner-city kids or something.

"Your kid's in that scout pack thing tonight, Tommy?"

"Troop. Pack is Cub Scouts. It's a Troop. And yeah."

Two stools away sits a man only legally allowed to drink for a couple of years now. He is called Dare on the streets. Dare is finishing his vodka and listening intently to the story of Jimmy Nose and the church.

Dare was most certainly never a Boy Scout.

***

46

Morning finds Mr. Brandt walking down into the boiler room of the Pierce Building to visit with The Mayor.

The Mayor is not in. Brandt closes his eyes in slight frustration, and shakes his head a little.

Brandt begins cleaning.

For the most part, The Mayor keeps himself contained to one small area of the boiler room. He tends to keep his area relatively clean, save for the books that are stacked up against most of the walls. Say what you will about the man, but The Mayor keeps his space clean.

The fact that The Mayor is out makes it easier for Brandt to make sure that everything is still on the up and up. As he cleans, he makes sure there is no evidence of illegal activity anywhere in the room. This is a part of the conditions for The Mayor's nesting of the boiler room. With the exception of that book The Mayor tracks things with...written in his own impossible language...he finds nothing out of the ordinary. If The Mayor is involved with crime, then he is also the world's foremost expert at stealth and cloaking.

As Mr. Brandt, the building superintendant, finishes straightening things and tucking away as many signs of The Mayor's presence in the Pierce Building as possible, the man himself returns to his boiler room.

He hovers at the doorway before entering his antechamber, and says, "Hello?" with more than a little uncertainty.

Once, there was an invader. Once, someone

came into his boiler room and started pushing The Mayor around until he gave up a few of his valuables. When he was dissatisfied with both the quality and quantity of The Mayor's valuables, he began to hit The Mayor. He hit The Mayor for about five minutes until his hands began to hurt. Then he kicked him twice and fled the building, never to be seen again.

The recovery process for The Mayor was long and difficult. When it was over, and he was released from St. Brigid, he came right back here to his boiler room.

He remembers the event all too clearly. The Mayor, needless to say, does not like surprises in his home.

"It's me, Mayor."

The Mayor comes into the boiler room the rest of the way. "Good morning, Mister Brandt."

He looks around the room.

"You've cleaned. You're here to tell me there's an inspection today, and I should make myself scarce."

"Yes. It's at 3 o'clock this afternoon, which means it will actually be at 1:45."

"Of course."

"And you know the drill."

"I do. Very well then. I will spend the day visiting the northeast side. I have people to visit there anyway."

"Thank you, Mayor."

"As always, thank *you*, Mr. Brandt. Thank you for your kindness."

***

"So what *is* it?"

Dare puts the lighter down and exhales. "I dunno."

Jay is seated above everyone else in the darkened room. An old school rap album is bumping in the background, just for noise. Jay has a girl sitting on either side of him, and is wearing enough gold to have a sore neck. He is the poster boy for inner-city gang youth from an 80's movie, right down to the product in his hair. He is also ruthless enough to kill without a thought, which is why none of the others in the room ever give him any crap about the way he dresses.

"Forget it," Jay growls. "Breakin' into a church to steal somethin' without knowing what it even is is stupid. A good way to get busted. People go crazy when you hit a church. 'Specially one on Seventeenth. I don't need no problems with The Mayor and his stinkys."

Dare is undeterred. "Maaaan. Alls I know is Jimmy Nose went in there to steal somethin'. Somethin' important or spendy enough that he didn't care about pissin' off who he work for. An' he didn't get it, an' now he gone."

"How you know he didn't get it?" Jay barks. "Preacher man said nothing missin'. Maybe he lyin'."

"Uh-uh," another boy says, a little emboldened after passing the lighter to someone else. "Father Vaughan ain't no liar. Not even to protect somethin'."

49

Jay rocks forward and falls back into his chair, waving a hand dismissively. "Whatever. Ya'll stay the hell away from that church until we know what's what. Dig?"

By way of acknowledgement, no one says anything.

The hunger is there. It is a fierce burning, a fiery stove in the hearth of her belly baking the hard bread of *need*. Her need is deep. Her time has worn quite thin.

The hunger has been there for as long as her memory serves, and her memory spans a long, long time. Eons.

Having someone to handle interference has made all the difference for her, as it did last time. He is particularly good at protecting her from any meddlers, as well. He also goes to great lengths to make sure she has a safe environment in which to grow stronger. Her last attempt at returning to this form was not nearly as successful as this time has already proven.

Still, there is the hunger. It rapidly approaches the point where she knows it will overtake her common sense. It will push her to do mindless things if she cannot keep it in check. In order to keep it at bay, she must keep up her strength. In order to build her strength...she must feed.

It is time to find more souls in need of judgment. It is time to expand the gift she has brought to her host. It is time to have the host take a more active role in making her stronger.

"So that just leaves the basement level," Mr. Brandt says to him as he presses the appropriate button on the elevator.

"Of course, the official report will take some time, but I have to tell you I'm very impressed with the current state of the building. You and your maintenance staff are to be commended for the upkeep of the Pierce."

"Thank you, sir," he says. The doors open and reveal the entry hallway for the maintenance basement level.

Slowly, Mr. Brandt the building manager and the inspector work their way around the basement. He touches things and looks at things and even takes a sniff of things and he makes little marks on a clipboard.

Mr. Brandt patiently waits. With the exception of the somewhat lived-in look of the boiler room, he knows he has nothing to worry about. The building is well cared for, and every inspection reflects this.

However, this is not the usual inspector. The usual inspector is visiting a sick relative somewhere downstate this week. This is someone new, a Mr. Carlton. He has never had to sweep the evidence of the Mayor aside for this person before, and he can only hope he has done a good enough job.

The boiler room is left for last, as if Mr. Carlton is building up as much stomach acid in Mr. Brandt as possible. Like a cheap two in the morning burrito made human and given a clipboard.

To the untrained eye, a glance at the boiler room would give no evidence of The Mayor's residence. Mr. Carlton peeks around for a bit and makes a very small notation on the clipboard.

"Does he stay here most nights?"

Gavin Brandt feels his stomach fall, and at first says nothing. Then, finally, he decides to comment. Denying it at this point would be foolish.

"I believe so. But I – "

"Relax, Mr. Brandt. I know all about him. I think what you do for him is commendable. My hope is that you aren't running a hotel beyond him."

"No sir, I am not."

"Then we're done here."

Brandt turns his head like a cat watching a fly. "Are we?"

"It's hot today. We've spent enough time in the boiler room. Let's go grab a coke and I can have you sign the review."

"I don't understand," Brandt says, worried that he might be belaboring the point and risks swinging the opinion in the other direction.

"There's nothing to understand." And he walks out into the hall towards the elevator, his blue suit attracting tiny specks of dust as he goes.

"Hello, Mr. Mayor."

The Mayor of Seventeenth Avenue is always happy to see The Proud Prince.

"How are things on the high floors, sir?"

"Another busy day. Never too busy for a lunch on my favorite bench, though. How are things on the basement floor?"

The Mayor sighs. "I wouldn't know, sadly. I'm out for the day. Inspection tour."

"Ah."

"How is *Killer Mine*?"

"Getting better. How is your busy day?"

"Not so bad, Proud Prince, but many things require my attention."

"So I hear."

The Mayor tilts his head, as if the inertia will help physically steer the conversation in an entirely fresh direction.

"And how are your grandsons, Proud Prince?"

Nicholas Prince blinks slowly. "Marcus is doing just fine."

"Good, good."

Nicholas closes his eyes and shakes his head slightly, once. "I have no idea how Darius is, not really. I'm still hoping he will make an effort to reach back in our direction. We both are. But he has to find his own way back."

***

The boy isn't stupid.

He knows the difference between a guy walking down the street minding his own business, and a gang banger. He doesn't see gang bangers on Seventeenth Avenue very often...but as he turns up Adrian's Alley without thinking...he realizes it was a huge mistake to do so. That the man who was leaning up against the wall of the front entrance to Honey's was up to no good and is about to ruin his evening. He just wanted to get back to his brownstone at Church and Eighteenth, and get the milk to his Mom. She's waiting for the milk. You never assume you're going to run into trouble on this street. At worst, you might find yourself being accosted by The Duck Man, or a couple of the cats in the alley. Or possibly old Buzzy if he's drunk and looking for the funds necessary to become *more so*.

The boy picks up his pace. For a split second, he considers breaking into a run.

"Don't," says the voice behind him. "Just don't."

The boy makes the curve of the alley, where the recyclables sit behind the Adrian Hotel, near the delivery doors. There aren't a lot of cars running up ahead on Eighteenth. He doesn't hear much in the way of foot traffic.

His arms are full, and he can't text anyone, which is bad enough for any teenager...let alone being followed by someone who is probably a West Side King.

Steam is rising from his head, so Dare pulls his hood over himself. The wind is starting to pick up, and even though it is summer, it is late enough in the evening that the breeze is a little chillier than he preferred without a hat on. The mountains are good at that, and the city sits right beside a few 12 or 13 thousand-foot peaks. The wind is blowing his dreadlocks around his face a bit as he walks up to the terrified kid.

"So, what do you know?"

The boy stops, and turns to face him.

Dare Prince is closer to him than he thought, and instinctively the boy finds himself backing away quickly. He trips over a wooden palate in the alley. Three cats jump in different directions when it skids and scrapes toward the wall until the boy falls on it, butt-first, looking up at the young man in the hood.

Adrian's Alley is quiet. The boy is wishing it could be a little more populated right now. The wish will be unfulfilled.

"I call out for The Mayor and your life on this street won't be worth spit, Dare."

Darius Prince looms over the boy, staring down at him with a crazed look on his face. He is fueled with rage, and booze, and whatever Jay was passing around earlier. There is something in his eyes that suggests the boy is best served saying nothing until he is addressed.

"The church," he says, coldly. "Spill it."

The boy looks around. There is still no one there to rescue him but a few cats lingering in the periphery, curious.

"Fine," he says, resolved to the fact that Dare is not going to let him get up until he gives him something useful to go on.

Dare's patience is beginning to wear even thinner.

"Well?" he demands, glaring.

"Father Vaughan went to Africa or somewhere not too long ago," the boy says, trying not to shake. "There's a rumor that he brought a special artifact or somethin' back, somethin' made of gold. I heard it was a knife."

"A golden knife? And it's hidden in the church somewhere?"

"That's what I hear."

In a rare moment of kindness, Dare reaches out a hand and helps the boy up. The boy takes it gingerly, unsure if he will be rising up into a knife or a fist or something.

"Wasn't so hard."

He gives the boy a smile.

The smile does not put the boy at ease. A second later, though, Dare turns and strolls casually back down to Seventeenth.

The boy finally understands the concept of what it is to feel your heart skip a beat. He's heard the saying before but never truly appreciated how accurately it describes the feeling.

He wipes his eyes, which he hadn't realized were full of tears. He picks up the bags and walks past the cats. Chairman Meow is one of them, and with his usual look of understanding and anthropomorphic intelligence…he stares down the alley at the form of Darius Prince.

Chairman Meow's yellow eyes narrow, and he glares at the man.

That is a bad man.

Bad men should stay out of his alley.

"You aren't going out again tonight, forget it."

Haley is drunk, as usual. She is Pete's third wife.

"I told you, I got business to take care of. I'm trying to figure out where Jimmy is."

She lights a cigarette and exhales her reply in a cloud of brownish-blue smoke. "Word on the street is Jimmy flaked. He scored something big at the church and he's on his way to California to look for his brother."

Pete stops in the middle of heading into the kitchen to get his keys. "Word on the *street*?"

"Yeah," she says, and flares her eyes at him. "The street."

He crosses back into the sitting room, and she takes another sip from her glass of gin.

"So, you're some great gangster moll now, is that it? You're tuned in to what's going on out on the street? You're talking about my business?"

"Knock it off, Pete," she says, getting up from the chair. "The wives talk. You know that. We have to have something to do. When we're not comparing how much more crap we have than each other. Or who our husbands might be spending their nights with."

"What?"

"You aren't in The Sopranos, you know."

He rolls his eyes angrily. "Oh shuuuut up. And you and the other wives are the best of pals now? You've been around for all of two months."

"Just because nobody likes *you* doesn't mean..."

His hand came out of nowhere, a fleshy bolt of lightning that struck her completely by surprise.

Haley has been hit by men before. She's even been hit by Pete before. She's biding her time , she tells herself. She'll be back on the road before too long, once she has everything she needs from this guy.

When he smacked her, she didn't even lose her grasp on her drink. He smacked her hard, like he did his previous wife. She didn't really even feel it. Honestly, she had to keep herself from smiling at the irony.

"I've asked you not to do that, Peter."

Pete doesn't like hearing her say "Peter." She says it the way the nuns at St. Ignatius did before he got kicked out and sent to Western High School.

He pulls his hand back up, pointing up with his index finger, as if he has a point to make.

She still hasn't rubbed her face where it stings. She looks him directly in the eyes and takes a sip of her gin.

Pete smiles at her and walks into the kitchen to grab his keys. He walks out of the front door without a further word.

She looks over at the door and makes a gun with her thumb and forefinger.

She drops the thumb.

"P'kew," she says, mimicking a shot and winking as if she were looking through an imagined gun sight.

Light from the hallway streams into the room as Zoey's Mom pulls open the door.

"What are you doing still up, young lady?"

"I can't sleep, Mama."

"How come?"

"Because everything's too interesting."

Her mother comes over to the bedroom window and gently kisses the top of her head.

"Everything's too interesting, huh?"

"Yep."

"What's so interesting?"

Zoey yawns in that wide-mouthed way only children can get away with. "Paper went into the shelter about an hour ago to be with his mom. Somebody was leaning up against the wall of First Methodist a little while ago. They were smoking. Smoking's bad."

"Yes. Yes it is."

"Smoking next to a church should be really bad."

"It probably is, yes." She rubbed Zoey's shoulders. "What else is goin' on out there?"

"Mr. Tanner from the first floor came home from Honey's about five minutes ago. He wasn't walking very good."

"Most people walking home from Honey's have that problem," she interjected.

"And the security company delivered something to the Porter Building right before you came in. See? The truck is still there!"

Zoey's mother looked up the street to the corner of Church & Seventeenth. A black GM Denali was parked out front with the engine running.

"Hmmm. Not bad, my little spy. But you need some sleep."

"Mom…"

"Summer is going to be over before you know it. You have to get back on a sleep schedule, baby. You'll have to sleep through the night to be able to do your very best when you go back to school. You want to do your very best, right?"

Zoey sighed. "Riiiiiight."

"Then you need some sleeping practice. I mean it. You've been staying up too late the last couple of weeks." She kisses the top of her blonde little head again.

"Bed, muskrat. Now."

She hugs her daughter, stands up, and closes the blinds.

Zoey climbs into her stuffed animal-laden bed. All manner of fake eyes stare out at the room around her, ever-vigilant for possible intruders and poised to strike with all their stuffing should danger present itself.

All of them, perhaps, except for the stuffed sloth she calls Pokey. Pokey has a cowardly look about him that suggests he would be useless in combat except for lying there with a look of stark terror on his face.

Her mother tucks her in, and Zoey closes her eyes with a smile.

As the door clicks shut, Zoey reopens her eyes. It isn't something she tries to do. It's just something that happens.

And it happens pretty much every night.

Pete Gravy checks the lock at the front of St. George's Catholic Church. It is, in fact, busted.

Sometimes, the world makes it too easy. If this was Jimmy's handiwork Pete is surprised. Jimmy's better than this.

He turns and looks up at the traffic camera. He smiles and waves at it because he isn't afraid to be seen on it. He has always been a more successful thief than people like Jimmy Nose because he knows how to look like he *belongs there.* No matter where *there* happens to be.

As he turns back around, he fails to notice that he is being watched by a snake, coiled in the darkness in the shadow of the church.

He walks into the entrance hall. The church is lovely. When he was a kid, it was huge and terrifying. It was supposed to be where he learned to fear God. Most of the kids he knew just learned how to fear the place itself. Your voice came back to you from the ceiling and the walls. The shadows played tricks on you. A hundred-year hall, filled with the ghosts of destitute settlers with nothing but their faith to sustain them. The murals on the walls, depicting scenes from the Bible, had these powerful eyes that followed you. No matter where you glimpsed them from.

His footsteps bounce back at him. He isn't afraid of the echoes and the shadows anymore. He smiles, and walks up to the office.

He searches for half an hour. There is nothing to be found that resembles a golden knife. His anger rises as his frustration boils. He turns off the flashlight and the lamp and sits in Father Vaughan's chair. It creaks and groans, being a relic all its own.

A faint sound in the silence draws his attention to the corner of the room. He listens to the darkness, and hears it again.

Laughter.

Soft but deep laughter.

It only takes a few seconds to realize it is coming from the cellar.

Pete grabs a baseball bat from the children's play area as he walks by.

Bottom of the ninth, Jimmy.

It waits in the silence, laughing. Wondering if they will continue to just *come* to him.

This is becoming so much simpler than it had anticipated.

The weather is rainy again today.

Paper is starting to wonder if the rain is ever going to stop falling. He coughs. The cough is becoming more prominent every day, and sounds more…wet.

He walks up Church Street from the women's shelter where his mother stays. Mom is not having a lucid morning, so he has decided to spend the entire day on Seventeenth going about his work. The stump where his right hand used to be itches, and he rubs it as he looks for a note from Zoey in the place where she usually deposits them.

No news at all. Unusual.

Maybe she actually fell asleep for once. He walks back to her building hoping to catch a glimpse of her.

There's no sign of her around the building, so he walks around Sang's bodega to the Newspaper Box across the street from St. George's and Sappia's delicatessen.

When he looks at Sappia's, which he does every morning as he gets his paper, he feels shame.

Every day, Paper gets his paper from this box. Sometimes, he has to wait for it. People in a hurry tend to slam the door of the box after they put in their 50 cents (or $1.50 on Sunday) and pull out their newspaper. However, if they slam the door, it doesn't close correctly and will open again if you carefully pull without pushing a little. Paper has never bought a newspaper from the good people at the Times-Dispatch.

It's locked right now, but he usually only has to wait in the little alley behind Zoey's building for a few minutes at this time of the day. Sure enough, after only a few minutes, a woman talking into a Bluetooth drops four bits into the slots, opens the old box, pulls out the Friday morning edition…and slams the door.

Paper collects his paper.

He walks back to Zoey's building, sits on the dry part of the sidewalk under the faded awning with his back to the brownstone, and reads. After all: Part of being *in the know* is knowing what everyone else knows.

He's reading the sports page when he hears the window open a few floors over his head.

"Hi, Paper."

He doesn't look up. "No notes from you. Slow night, or are you grounded again?"

"Grounded again. I saw someone go into the church last night and Mom caught me trying to go get a peek at him."

He steps out from under the awning to get a better look at her. Raindrops lap at his cheeks as he looks up at her, a naïve Romeo to her innocent Juliet.

"First Meth, or St. George?" He gestures over to the First Methodist Peace Temple across the street.

She frowns down at him, clearly bored after only a few hours of forced incarceration. Zoey is the sort who has to roam free.

"Same church. St. George's. I think it was Pete Gravy. I'm not sure if he left or not. Mom kept coming in to check on me, so I had to stay in bed. I fell asleep after a while."

"Hang on," Paper says, and he climbs up on a trash can to reach the ladder for the fire escape. It's a scene straight out of a 1950's movie, or would be, if he had on a porkpie hat.

Paper takes the fire escape stairs to the window in her mother's room, next to Zoey's. "I suppose you aren't aware that I have plenty of other eyes on the street, and you are *allowed* to get some sleep every now and then."

She smiles. "I know."

"You have to delegate. Do you know what delegate is?"

"Not really." She shrugs.

"It means get some help. I have two other kids who can work Church & Seventeenth during the night and overnight. Let them take up the slack, okay?"

"Okay." She seems sad, and Paper knows why. He rests the stump of his missing hand against her shoulder.

"You have not let me down at all. You could never do that. I should have known that you would have done this job all hours of the day and night."

"Uh-huh."

"Don't get yourself in trouble; don't make yourself sick because you aren't sleeping. I appreciate you and you are important. That's why I need to know that you are at your best and taking care of yourself, okay?"

"Okay."

The window next to Paper slides up. "Hi, Paper!"

"Hello, ma'am."

"Zoey can't play today."

"She was just telling me that, ma'am." He is

already climbing down, carefully.

"Paper," she says, "come in through the window and use the hallway. I don't want to worry about you falling."

"Yes ma'am."

He climbs in through the window, and she closes it behind him. As they leave her bedroom and pass Zoey's room, there is a muffled "Bye, Paper," in a sad little squeak from the other side of the door.

Paper looks at Zoey's mother and they smile at each other.

"Her imprisonment should be over with in time for her to come out to play after dinner. Just keep an eye out for her and keep her out of trouble."

"Always, ma'am."

She always likes how he calls her *ma'am*.

At the end of the hall, instead of turning towards the door, she waves a finger toward the kitchen. She opens the cookie jar and holds it out at Paper.

Paper dips his left hand in and fishes out a nice, big chocolate chip.

"Take two," she says, and he obeys.

"Try to convince her to take it easy, Paper. She's having a lot of trouble sleeping and I think she's really stressed out. She's only 8 years-old. She shouldn't be so stressed out."

He hasn't noticed, but she has poured a small glass of milk, and put a little plate in front of him to set his cookies on.

"So what do you want me to...?"

"…I want you," she interrupts, "to get her to play and be a kid. I trust you, Paper, because I watch the way you are with all the kids in this neighborhood. A lot of us parents do. We know that the kids…kind of *work* for you, getting information to The Mayor."

Paper swallows. "You *do?*"

"We do."

"Oh."

"None of us interfere because you keep the kids busy. You keep them out of harm's way and out of trouble. You're a good kid. That's why I knew I could talk to you like an adult. I suspect you're far more mature than you should be. Things haven't exactly been easy for you, have they?"

Paper swallows again. He suspects she is pausing at exactly the wrong moments because she finds it amusing somehow.

"No. they haven't."

Zoey's mother fishes a cookie out for herself. "They haven't been easy for Zo, either. Remember that." She holds out the jar. "Make sure you grab a couple for the road."

Paper spots Father Vaughan coming out of the church.

"Paper! Come here, son."

He is always more than a little leery of people who call him *son*. He crosses Seventeenth Avenue while chewing the last of a cookie, and smiles at the priest as he finishes chewing and swallows. Zoey's mother is an exceptional baker.

"Good morning, Father."

"What's the word, Paper?"

After a moment of internal debate, he responds. "Treasure, Father. That's the word of the day."

"Is that right?"

"Treasure."

"What treasure is this?"

Paper walks over to the doors and traces the busted lock with the fingers of his left hand. "Supposedly, it's a treasure *you* are hiding here at St. George's."

Father Vaughan crosses his arms. He's sweating in his thick black shirt. Summer is a horrible time to be a priest.

"Is that right? A treasure?"

"A treasure."

"What kind of..."

Paper interrupts. "Word is that you have a precious item from somewhere exotic, something with magical properties. Smart money says it's a golden knife or something."

The priest purses his lips. "It must be pretty well hidden, then. Because I know every inch of this magnificent old building. I know where all of the antiquities are located, not that there are many. I know where all the secret passages are. And I can tell you, my news-knowing little friend, that the location of anything that valuable or mystical eludes me. Because it isn't there."

"Good to know," Paper says.

"Maybe you can start spreading that around a bit."

"I think I can do that, Father. However, remember one thing. People will believe what they decide they are gonna believe."

"Yes," Father Vaughan says. "They certainly will."

Paper shrugs.

"However," Father Vaughan continues, "I am a man who is thankful that people believe in things. It's kind of how I make my living, after all."

He throws Paper a wink and a smile.

"Yeah, that's true," Paper laughs.

"Do you believe in God, Paper?"

Questions like this always make his stump itch. He rubs it absent-mindedly.

"Well," he says. "Does it count that I want to?"

Father Vaughan smiles. "I suppose it's a start, son.

The City Council bowed to the pressure of public opinion a year ago and installed a skateboard park at Grove Park. It sits on the park's west corner, at Eighteenth Avenue and Port Street. All day long here in the middle of summer, there are skaters using it. They use it with one simple understanding…skating stays in the skate park. Anyone boarding in any other part of Grove Park will find themselves responsible for the park closing for the rest of that day.

It made the thought of a skate park more palatable for the city council and sounds like a great deterrent. The problem, though, is that it isn't enforced very well. There is almost never a cop in Grove Park. There is usually no need for law enforcement this close to Seventeenth Avenue and the hospital. Crime doesn't usually darken these particular streets.

Paper is sitting in the park rereading today's Times-Dispatch when he notices The Proud Prince walking out of the Pierce building. City Bus 8117 rolls up Grove Street and squeaks to a halt at the bus stop at Grove and Seventeenth. Paper coughs particularly hard, and it proves productive. He spits behind the nearest tree.

The rain finally decided to let up again about two hours ago, and the heat of late morning has done a fine job of drying things up today. For that reason, young Marcus Prince and two of his friends have ridden the bus to Grove Park to skate away a very boring Friday. You can only play so many videogames for so long before your body insists on some form of additional stimulation.

For Marcus, it is a chance to hang out with his Grandfather, as well.

The man The Mayor always refers to as The Proud Prince is Nicholas Prince. He's the Vice President in charge of International Accounts at Proud Marketing Group in the Pierce Building, where The Mayor lives.

Prince has spent most of the last six years being a "single Grandparent". He had been raising his grandsons Darius and Marcus until Darius left his home at 17 to run with a gang called The West Side Kings under the name Dare.

Obsessed with making sure his other grandson wouldn't follow the same path, Nicholas Prince has poured most of his energy into Marcus. He continues to try to reach out to Darius, but he never responds.

Paper and his network of kids have passed several messages along to Dare. Dare has ignored them all.

The Mayor likes The Proud Prince. Prince is a voracious reader, finishing a book every three days or so. As he finishes paperbacks, he passes them along to The Mayor. Because he reads faster than the man who benefits from his generosity, The Mayor's ersatz domicile is filled with stack after stack of used paperbacks. He often gives them away as gifts, for fear they will collapse eventually and bury him.

The Proud Prince sees Marcus disembark from the 8117 Bus and waits for him to cross over to him at the city block that comprises Grove Park. He gives his 13 year-old grandson a hug and a kiss on the top of his head.

"Have fun.," he says to the boys. "I'll be back with lunch in about a half-hour. Don't ride your boards to the skate park."

"We know," Marcus says. To their credit, the boys don't hop on their boards until the skate park is actually in sight a minute later. By that point, The Proud Prince is waiting for the light to cross Church Street and grab some sandwiches from

Pete's Hoagies for himself and the boys.

As Prince walks past the ornate and beautiful St. George's Church, about a half-a-block from his destination...he catches sight of his other grandson.

Dare is standing at the black iron fence around the outdoor tables in front of Sappia's. He and another boy are flirting with a pair of Italian girls eating their lunches, wishing they could be left alone.

He says nothing as he softly walks up behind him, and says, "Your brother really misses you."

The young man standing next to Dare has never seen his friend's face go white in the way it just did.

Dare doesn't say anything. The girls who were eating at the table, knowing a good break when they see one, grab their lunches and go back into the intermittent air conditioning of Sappia's dining area.

"He's over at the skate park," Nicholas Prince says. "You should really go over and say hello to him while he's down here."

Dare's friend is looking back and forth at Dare and the bald man in the suit who is talking to him. Back and forth, like he's watching the world's smallest tennis match. Except Dare hasn't returned a serve yet.

Darius Prince continues to look straight ahead, not saying a word. His face is without expression. He is aware of that, and he isn't sure if it's because he's ashamed of the way he's acted, or he doesn't want to look weak in front of his friend.

"Cool," he finally says. He says it briskly without any trace of emotion whatsoever.

Nicholas Prince heaves a sigh and walks along the storefronts between himself, Pete's Hoagie Shop & Party Store, and the intersection of Seventeenth and Sawyer.

The Proud Prince does not feel particularly proud when he thinks about the myriad ways he seems to have failed his grandson, and by proxy, their late father.

Dare and his friend walk up Church Street to Eighteenth, and then turn toward the mountains. They pass Grove Park, and Dare spots his baby brother learning new tricks on his old skateboard from a couple of older boys.

"Tell Jay I'll be up there in a minute."

His friend walks on without him, and Dare walks over to the park.

He stands there for a bit before Marcus glances in his direction and notices him watching him. He drops his board and rolls over to his older brother, running right into him and hugging him.

"Where the hell you been at?"

"That's how you talk?" Dare says, and he hugs his brother back.

They talk to each other for 10 minutes before Darius begins to fall apart on the inside. He doesn't want to show any kind of weakness or remorse to his little brother, so he promises to see him more often and walks towards Port Street.

Marcus slumps in sadness, just in time for his grandfather to walk up beside him and drop a hand on his shoulder.

"Hey, Champ," he says. "I got you double-meat and barbecue chips."

Marcus wipes his eyes and hugs his granddad.

Nicholas Prince has just decided to take the rest of the afternoon off.

Friday night at Honey's means drinking.

It means every sport in season on nearly two dozen flatscreen TVs that the owner practically had to mortgage his house for. It means the kitchen has two extra people working in it.

It means a number of cars still in the lot Saturday morning and a lot of cab fares. It means a fair amount of people coming to collect their cars while wearing the same clothing in the blinding sunlight of Saturday. Except this weekend when it is supposed to be cloudy. For most of the afflicted that isn't going to make much of a difference. Hung over is as hung over does.

For some reason tonight, Friday night at Honey's means…religion.

A man clad all in black walks in and sits down around half past 10. He is somewhat non-descript, and no one really notices him but Amy behind the bar. It's Amy's job to notice the people who walk into Honey's though, and there is nothing particularly remarkable about the man when he arrives.

He orders a glass of Merlot, and pays with cash. He says nothing at all. When Amy addresses him, he replies with a nod. However, he looks around the room in a way that makes her very uncomfortable. It brings to mind the way the tigers at the zoo look at the children on the other side of the thick glass.

Amy is pouring his second glass when he makes disturbing, penetrating eye contact with her. She feels like he is looking right through her.

"Tell me, Miss," he says. "Are you even aware?"

Amy cocks a painstakingly drawn eyebrow.

"Am I aware of...what?"

"Are you aware that the devil's servant has come to your city?"

Amy finishes pouring and sets the bottle down. She begins wiping the counter as she says "The devil's servant. Is that right?"

"It is," the man replies.

He is dressed head to toe in black, wearing a black trench coat without a belt...far more clothing than one really needs in the summer, even in the mountains. His hair, also black, is slicked back and tied in a tight ponytail. It serves to push his entire face forward, and adds depth to the wild stare of his eyes.

"Wouldn't know him if I saw him," she says, and walks to a customer at the other end of the bar who is waving a 10 dollar bill over his head as he leans forward and looks at her with a smile.

"I think you might," he mumbles, and the person at the stool to his right gets up and leaves. The patron to his left gives him a look.

The sportscaster on the wide television

screen directly above them, over the bar, continues to stare at them, oblivious. He drones on and on about someone's ACL tear and what affect it might have on his team's season. He is on Mute. No one in the room really cares, with the possible exception of an odd patron or five who might happen to have him on their fantasy team or something.

Someone else sits to the man in black's right, bumping him slightly in the process.

"Sorry, bro."

The newcomer tosses a pack of Winston Lights on the bar and waits for Amy.

Amy finishes up on the other end of the bar and spots the new arrival. She pours a very tall Coors Light into a glass and walks it over to him. She knows his order. She knows the order of at least 85% of the people in Honey's tonight. It's her job to know the usual of the usuals.

She writes his beer on a ticket and turns it upside-down in front of him.

"Howya doin', Bry?"

"Good, sweetheart. How's that kid?"

"Stewie's fine," she says. "Had a cold last weekend. He's over it."

"The devil's servant has come and must be destroyed!"

The man in black has finished his second glass of wine and shouted this quite suddenly.

"Dude," the man at his left says.

"I got this," Amy tells him. "Look, Mister...?"

"He comes in the guise of an angel! He speaks of beauty and truth with the tongue of impurity and insidious lies!"

In the area near the bar, people have fallen out of their own conversations all-around him. Most of them are starting to back away. One especially skittish and uncomfortable couple makes a beeline straight for the exit.

"Okay, let's go." The voice is that of Craig, the bouncer. The fists that have balled up the collar and back of the ranting man's coat are Craig's, as well. Amy, who had wisely retreated, is slowly moving back to that part of the bar.

"Each of you will feel it soon! You fail to understand the gravity of this situation! You need to realize that the devil's servant has come, and if you do not act to stop it, you are all..."

Craig has pushed the front doors open with his right foot.

"...in the gravest of danger! I have come to save you all!"

Craig hurls the man like a black-clad duffel onto the rain-slicked sidewalk. The man lands at the feet of Tommy, who is looking to grab a drink at his favorite watering hole after a meeting that ran late with one of his associates.

Tommy and Craig look at each other for a moment and share a smile.

"You will all perish!" the man shouts. He has not bothered to pick himself up yet and lies somewhat still on the concrete.

"Long night, Craig?"

"Hey man, how ya doin'? This guy's been bothering people, talking about the devil or somethin'. Come on in."

Tommy steps over the man, who suddenly twists and grabs Tommy's ankle. Tommy fights to keep his balance, and makes eye contact with the man clinging to the bottom of his leg.

"You can help me destroy the devil's servant, Tommy! Together we will uncover the horrible fate that has already touched your city, before it sprea- "

Tommy works his foot free and kicks the man hard across the face with his designer shoe.

"Listen, you. First of all…don't EVER touch me."

He emphasizes the point of the word "ever" with another shot to the man's face. He rolls over and holds his nose, finally starting to get to his knees in an early attempt at getting up off the sidewalk.

"Second, if you got some preaching to do…save it. We get plenty of it in this neighborhood. We get it every Sunday, right down that street over there in about ten different buildings. And they've already got holy men on the job at each one."

"You need not be in league with the Beast, Tommy," the man says. He rises, and blood begins to pour out of his nose.

Tommy has heard enough and walks into the bar. He spots Amy at the bar and gives her a smile.

Amy smiles back. Pete Gravy was not her only meal ticket in this neighborhood.

Craig turns around and follows him back into Honey's.

"You are all doomed!" the strange man shouts, as people walk past him rather quickly. "You..."

His attention is suddenly diverted by a snake slithering past him, winding its way up to Church Street.

His eyes go wild with righteous indignation as he leans down at it and screams...

"I KNOW WHAT YOU'RE UP TO!!!"

He proceeds to preach with great zeal to everyone who approaches Honey's.

Word of this reaches the ears of Craig, thanks to a few customers who pushed their way past the man.

Craig and the manager walk through the entrance to *gently convince* the man that he really needs to move along.

They stop at the doorway.

The Mayor is talking to the man in black, and has pointed in the direction of Church Street.

The man in black nods, hangs his head for a moment, and heaves a sigh so full that his entire body cocks like a shotgun. All at once, he lifts his head, and he walks away.

The manager puts a hand on The Mayor's shoulder.

"Thanks."

"Don't mention it." He looks over the man's shoulder. "Evening, Craig."

"Good evening, Mayor. Buy you a beer? We owe you one after that."

"No, but I could go for a Pepsi. I haven't had a Pepsi in some time, and could really go for one."

"I'll be right back," the manager says.

The Mayor leans into Craig's ear.

"Call the Police, Craig. That man had a rather sizeable knife hidden on him, with a brown and gold handle."

Craig nods and pulls up his cell phone. The speed dial is already working to connect the call.

Friday night goes on without any further excitement, unless you apply the definition to the activities that went on after midnight in the apartment of Amy the bartender.

By that time, Sergeant Zachary has informed Craig that there is absolutely no sign whatsoever of the mysterious street preacher in black, or his large knife.

At a little after one in the morning, Tommy gets in his car and starts it up. Classical music flows out of the speakers, as always.

It isn't until now as he's leaving Amy's place and heading home to his wife that Tommy starts to wonder what it was. Something about his encounter with the strange man in front of Honey's is bothering him.

Since boyhood, Tommy has been blessed with an exceptional memory. He is replaying the order of events as he drives. Over and over again in his head he pictures everything exactly as it happened...trying to figure out what it is that bothers him about it.

It takes only a few minutes for him to finally realize what it is.

He's pretty sure Craig never said his name when they were outside with the man in black. He knows he never said his name around the man. He knows no one else said it either.

He is equally sure the strange man called him Tommy.

"Ya'll are scared."

Dare spits the words at them with the fire of a peer. A peer who knows he can't do something alone, and the best way to marshal a force together is through the use of shame.

"Shut up, Dare.

"Ain't nobody gonna be watchin' the place. Ain't nobody gonna be home. Easy pickin's. We in, we search the office 'cause it gotta be in there, and then we out. Easy."

"Easy," one of the other two boys at the table repeats. He says it with the tone of someone who would just as soon believe that the moon is going to melt tonight in the August heat. "If it so damn cut and dry and easy like that, why Jay tell us *no*? Why he say stay away from the church?"

Dare lights a cigarette. "Hell, I don' know, Dime. Maybe he got religion or somethin'. Maybe he wanna wait and get whatever it is for hisself."

The youngest kid, 16 year-old Be, takes off his hat and runs his fingers through his own hair for a few seconds before placing the hat carefully back on his head. He has never been to Oakland, but he wears a Raiders hat. "Maybe we go get the damn thing an' we give it to Jay. Move up in the peckin' order."

Dare and Dime look over at him and smile.

"All right then," Dare says. "We do this. We do this tonight."

Dime shakes his head. "Uh-uh. Cops still hanging around the church. We let it cool a couple days. *Then* we do what we gotta do."

Young Be nods his head in a vigorous fashion. He nods in the sycophantic way followers always do when they are blessed with a delay for something they didn't want to do in the first place.

Dare looks Be over carefully. It wasn't that long ago that he was the young kid, hoping for a shot at being a part of something like this. Something that could be *huge*. Be isn't the smartest kid in the Kings but he shows a lot more promise than Babyface does. He's the perfect third set of hands for something like this.

He can tell, here in the quiet, that she is truly with him right now. Something in her eyes today is typically absent from them. Now is the time.

"You remember, right Mom? You have to remember."

She says nothing at first. After a handful of seconds something sparks in the dark pitch of her eyes, and she pulls Paper closer to her.

"I remember, baby. Some things are gone, but the things that matter most are burned too deep to ever be washed away."

Paper nestles into her sweatshirt, which bears the name and logo of the city's NFL team.

"So, tell me."

Paper's mother breathes a heavy sigh. She looks down and kisses the top of Paper's head. Far more is said with the kiss than she would ever be able to say to him with words. Words are her failure. She has never been particularly good at them.

She heaves a sigh, and her bosom pushes him away before pulling him back in. Moments like this with her son are few and far between. He spends far more time on the street than he does here with her in the shelter. She blames herself for that, because she is convinced the fault is hers.

For a full minute, they hold each other in silence, mother and son. In every second of that minute, she debates whether she should tell her son everything. At the same time, she admonishes herself for never having done so. Has she been protecting her husband, or her son? For that matter, why does she still subconsciously refer to him as her husband? Is she still expecting him to sweep in through the doors of the shelter, beg her to take him back, and afford her the opportunity to live happily ever after?

Yes. She does.

Pathetic, she thinks to herself.

Suddenly flushed with anger and righteous indignation, she decides the time has come. Lord knows when she will be lucid enough again to relay this information to him anyway.

"You were five," she begins, and then pauses to purse her lips. "Five when your Dad met her."

"What was her name?" he interrupted.

"I don't remember," she lies. "They worked together. A lot of late evenings that started out as work and eventually became something else."

She pauses. Paper feels like he is expected to say something. He doesn't know what it should be, so he says nothing, waiting. His mother pours some water from a pitcher and takes a drink of it. The cold water hurts her bad teeth, but feels good on her sore throat. Fair trade-off.

"He said...he *said*," she spat, still clearly insulted by the idea, "that he felt *comfortable* with her. That I *exhausted* him. I had too much baggage. I told him he shouldn't talk about you like that..."

She stops herself, realizing what she is saying to him. Paper fights back the dropping of a tear.

"He told me you had nothing to do with the baggage. He said I drove him to her. I didn't understand what it was to be a wife anymore, or a lover. You really want to hear all of this?"

Paper rubs the back of his head. "Maybe not *all* of it, mom."

If she hears him, his words fail to register with her. She is off to the races now.

"But he didn't understand that I was under a lot of pressure and a lot of stress I mean between losing my job at Nero's and then when my mother got sick and I had to spend all that time in Billings with her because God forbid my goddamn sisters do anything to help take care of her and with him having to go out of town the weekend of the funeral and I had to take you to Montana and explain death to you which was not easy because you were too little to grasp it and you broke our hearts when you wanted to know why Grammy wouldn't wake up to play Uno with you and..."

He can see in her eyes that the spark is gone again. And so is she.

He holds her close, and he listens to her rambling until it stops. He doesn't really hear it, but he is holding her close, and he is listening.

For the most part that seems to be the most important thing he can be doing at this moment.

A cold night's wind sweeps into the alley.

A snake slithers into Adrian's Alley from Seventeenth Avenue, as if it lacks a direction. In truth, it is disoriented and confused. It rolls up on a collection of the alley's cats under a high, thin light that shines on the puddle-filled alley. The cats scatter in different directions. All but one of them, anyway.

Chairman Meow stands his ground and leans down at the intruder into his alley. He stares the snake into a stalemate and puffs out his tail in a display of dominance.

The other cats stare from the sidelines as Chairman Meow circles the strange little creature. Chairman Meow is a very worldly and wise cat, but he isn't familiar with what this is. It looks like a tail that lacks both fur and an ass to hang in front of. It appears to be intelligent, and it smells unusual.

Chairman Meow begins to raise his hackles and growl, and then stops suddenly.

The snake has made no moves at all since stopping before the clowder of cats. It stares at Chairman Meow, and the large cat suddenly stops making any noise at all.

His tail returns to normal, the arch softens in his back, and he stares back. The two animals seem to understand each other on some level, and the other cats begin to emerge from the darkness they had all melted into, the better to see what was going on.

The snake coils itself around Chairman Meow's legs for a moment, and then slithers off toward Eighteenth Avenue.

The great cat turns to his right and takes a few steps toward his usual sleeping spot. As he does so, he can't help but notice that his sore leg, tweaked a bit while jumping from somewhere high up recently, no longer bothers him.

The Mayor of Seventeenth Avenue was not yet awake.

He dreamed of camping in the woods, away from the urban sprawl. Just he and…the *others*.

The identity of the others was unclear again tonight. They usually existed in his dreams as a tangle of disembodied voices, all murmuring together just out of the view of his mind's eye. There was a woman. There was a child. They were all laughing and having a great time. The Mayor never has any idea who these people are, or why they insist on taking a starring role in his sleep every now and then.

Their appearances were equally confusing and comforting when they occurred. Usually it was more of the latter than the former. He felt oddly at peace with these nocturnal visitors.

Their identities are not the only mystery. No one knows The Mayor's true name either, including The Mayor himself.

As The Mayor slept, he was oblivious to the sudden burst of light that filled the vast space that served as his bedchamber. The Mayor usually slept here in the boiler room of the Pierce Building. It was a 40-story gleaming tower of glass and steel nestled in the south corner of Grove Street and Seventeenth Avenue. It was a lot of office space. It included the global headquarters of a major North American financial player, three floors of medical offices, and a pair of radio stations that still employed actual people in them.

Sleeping in the corner of the boiler room, the equipment in the corridor throws long, hard shadows at The Mayor as he rolls over to face away from the bright blue light. The room remains silent as the light moves closer to the spot where he sleeps. He snores lightly, as if the noise is a secret.

Draw up your strength.

At the center of the light is a hazy circle, something like a patch of glazed glass made into liquid. It rolls and rotates like a lightly opaque and gassy planet swimming in methane at the edge of a solar system throwing the light of a star into the small space. The light moves deliberately like a living thing.

My ally has crossed over. I can feel it. I will need your help. Heavy is the head that wears the crown.

It arcs gracefully around the backup boiler to the spot where The Mayor lies nestled in his bed of appropriated shelter blankets. The Mayor's grubby stuffed rabbit, Mister Winkles, is tucked under his bony right arm. The light reflects in Mister Winkles' black plastic eyes, and it gives his plush face a look childish innocence and wonder, as if he were living in a cartoon.

The meek shall inherit the Earth.

The light hovers back and forth like a pendulum as The Mayor snores lightly, dreaming of the park, the voices, and a sunny day's picnic.

Rest now.

The light does this for about a minute, and then goes out all at once. The room is dark and still.

The Mayor finally begins to stir as Mister Winkles stares into the darkness.

Everyone calls the boy Paper for a reason.

Paper is already awake this morning. He is coughing again, and he has started the day's work.

It is through the efforts of Paper that The Mayor keeps his power centralized and is given the amount of time needed to dispense the correct wisdom to keep his people moving in the right direction. Paper also serves as the go-between, and the personal secretary for The Mayor. Paper does a lot for someone so young.

No rumor lives on the Seventeenth, and no *important* crime befalls a victim without Paper knowing about it. No loud scene with shouts and tears and bald-faced lies and hurt feelings occurs between troubled lovers…without Paper knowing about it.

A minimum of twice per day, Paper makes his way to the boiler floor of the Pierce Building to report to The Mayor of Seventeenth Avenue *all that is new.* He briefs The Mayor when the man rises in the morning, and he is there to tuck his wise old benefactor in at night.

As breaking news warrants, of course, Paper's plentiful network of street miscreants spring into action as information runners. Paper's kids are all slightly younger than he. Most of them are under 10, actually. They comprise his own, private, Homeless Twitter: an informational river funneling the latest information to Paper and The Mayor, to ensure that the official business proceeds unabated.

Paper is missing his right hand.

He and his mother were evicted from their home when Paper was seven years old. His father had disappeared and his mother was too proud at first to accept charity from anyone. Paper remembers the empty feeling in his heart the day he found out their little house would no longer be the place where he lived. How it felt watching the ants play about the thin, strangling weeds that lined the sides of the sidewalk that led to the front door. No matter how hard they had tried to do battle with the ants and weeds, both came back every year. It seemed unfair to him that the people had to go and the ants and weeds got to stay.

Eventually, Mommy ended up at the women's shelter just southeast of Seventeenth on Church Street. Although Paper technically lived there, too, he spent nearly all of his time on and around Seventeenth. He spent his nights at the shelter with his mother because the law forced him to. She was usually asleep when he left each morning and asleep when he came back at night. In the early days, she slept a lot.

He had grown up a lot in the last five or six years. Enough to know what chronic depression was. Better than most, he was aware of what it looked like. He kissed it on the forehead twice a day.

A few years ago, when he was about to turn 10, Paper pinched a bundle of steaks from the butcher counter at Sappia's. This was not the malicious act of a young street criminal or a prank fueled by rage or even a cry for help. This was the spontaneous decision of a loving son who wanted his mother to have a nice birthday dinner: burn-barrel steaks at the ends of cleanly whittled sticks. Mommy would venture into Seventeenth Avenue with him sometimes and warm herself in Adrian's Alley with the people among whom Paper spent his day.

Paper respected Mister Sappia, and felt bad about stealing the meat. He also managed to do this without the old man seeing him, and for a minute thought he was going to get away with it.

People saw him around all the time. No one would ever suspect him of theft. Paper was always honest.

The nephew Vinny, however, saw him do it. Vinny had just placed the steaks on the counter for a delivery he was to make in a few minutes time. As he locked eyes with Paper, who was backing toward the door, he whipped off his butcher's apron and vaulted over the high counter. He was an exceptional athlete at Westside High School, something Paper thought about all-too-late, as he bolted out of the door.

Vinny raced after Paper without either of them having said a word, his little paper hat clinging desperately to his head as he pursued the terrified child up Seventeenth avenue. Mister Sappia poked his head though the window in time to see Vinny slip out of the entrance as fast as he could make the turn onto the sidewalk.

Paper ran without a single thought other than escape. Intending to hide somewhere in the alleys around Church and Grove Streets, he had turned left instead when leaving the entrance to Sappia's. This took him directly to the crossing of Seventeenth and Sawyer. Thanks to poor planning by the city's founders more than a century before, the intersection was also the exact spot where the railroad tracks crossed Seventeenth, running due north and south. The city's founders were also guilty of Northwest-to-Southeast streets and Northeast-to-Southwest avenues on the west side. The advantage to this was less chance of being blinded by the sun when driving down the street.

It made maps of the city look odd, though, when you looked at the west side of Downtown at the edge of the mountains. There was a strange, striped-diamond shape wrapped around the hulking manse of St. Brigid Regional Hospital.

Clutching the bundle tightly to his chest, Paper was oblivious to everything else around him as the adrenaline stoked the panic in his heart and directed his feet to carry him through the intersection. Fortunately, for him, no cars were passing through it now. He ran around the lowered crossing arms of the train tracks.

Equally focused on the chase was Vinny. Vinny was a superb athlete, a scholarship winner who was preparing to ride his swift feet to the State University. Vinny Sappia was unaccustomed to losing a race of any kind. He was going to get those steaks back. He had no intentions of hurting the boy who grabbed them, but that wouldn't keep him from putting a little fear in him first.

Vinny also ran around the gates, his mind scarcely registering the sharp sound of the loud horn as he stepped over the rail sunk into the pavement.

Directly into the path of the 4:15 Blue Line train.

Paper managed to slip off the line before it flattened him. The steaks fell free of his left hand, dropping out of his grasp as he jumped across the tracks. He spun his right hand behind him to try to catch them…purely a reactive movement…and was surprised for a split-second to see the blur of the train.

In the same glance, he saw Vinny's eyes go wide as the train slammed into him, full-bore.

The shock of seeing Vinny struck down by the Blue Line created a full two-second pause before Paper realized that his own arm had caught the edge of the train, too.

The impact knocked Paper backward, and he rolled under the crossing gate into Sawyer Street. Copious amounts of blood trailed down the pavement with him. He rolled to a stop under the wheel of an idling Ford Bronco, whose driver had already slammed it into park and was exiting the driver's side door.

Paper's hand had been severed at the wrist by the train, and it took almost five full seconds for Paper to realize it was gone. The story goes that Paper's first scream carried all the way to Fifty-First Avenue and Port on the far Northwest corner of the city. If not for the hospital being on the same end of Seventeenth, Paper would likely have bled to death quickly. As luck would have it, some of The Mayor's people carried him to the ER Ambulance bay at St. Brigid Regional. He was unconscious by the time they rushed him through the automatic doors in a phalanx of excited voices.

Vinny had died instantly and horribly. No one but Paper would ever know why he had been chasing the younger boy. Paper nearly died from blood poisoning after his wound was sealed. After returning to the street, he never stole again. The disastrous flirtation with it would forever be his only attempt at thievery. In fact, he admonished any of his young informers who ever dared to do so. Old man Sappia never spoke another word to Paper, convinced there was more to Vinny's death than he was aware and that the boy knew it well. Paper mourned Vinny from a distance at the funeral.

Paper's mother drank herself mad over the course of the next year or so, and The Mayor took the boy in, giving him title to the unused utility shed behind the Pierce Building. It made for a good base of operations for the lad. The Mayor ran Seventeenth Avenue and knew a quality employee when he saw one, no matter how many hands they might have.

By the end of that summer, Paper was back at the important work of reporting the living news of Seventeenth Avenue.

This morning, three years after the accident, Paper kissed his sleeping mother's forehead and pulled on his shoes. He slipped quietly into the hallway, and strolled through the front doors of the women's shelter. The doors were heavy and pushing them open with a hand and a stump was always a challenge. The way he saw it *everything* worth doing was a challenge.

He walked across Church Street and began checking the places where his Paperboys (and sole Papergirl) left their notes for him. It appeared to have been a quiet night. He is hopeful it will be a quiet day, as well. He isn't feeling very well, and needs some mothering. Perhaps she'll be up for some today.

He takes a deep breath of air and begins walking along Seventeenth toward the shed beside the alley that ran behind the Pierce Building.

A rumble of thunder chased a flash of light, and the rain began coming down hard once again.

Paper coughed again and dropped his head against the wet.

Geneva, some time ago.

The Black Death has arrived here finally and has depleted both the supplies and the spirit of the brilliant doctors in the city. This has been an impressive piece of work, given that Geneva has one of the most advanced-thinking schools of medicine in all of Europe.

The plague started slowly and the first round of preventive inoculations did a fair job of leveling off the number of reported cases. Puffed up with their success, a number of doctors have taken to horseback to spread the word and the vaccine to the neighboring cities in an effort to see if it can be useful.

This was the idea of the government. However, it has proven short-sighted.

A week has come and gone and the second wave of infection is washing over the city. At least half of the doctors and medical students are in the field now, and those who remain are unable to turn the tide.

People are dying all over the city, and they are dying horribly.

Doctor Von Hanley, a brilliant professor from

Amsterdam, has treated at least a hundred people today and is starting to notice a serious dip in his own energy.

He is a wise man, and an exceptional doctor. He is one of the leading medical minds of the day, and he knows better than almost anyone in the world what is at work in his body. There is softness in his arm muscles that he is unable to move past. He can feel a deep congestion welling up in his lungs. He is not worried about it. He has already come to accept it. He simply wants to accomplish as much as possible before he is no longer able to perform the role God has asked of him.

The same is true of the man in black armor who was assisting him this morning. He only wants to perform his duty. It is a sacred duty that God has tasked him with. He has had the privilege of looking into the face of God. Not the metaphorical face, like witnessing the opening of a flower or the rising of the sun over the peaks of Bavaria. He has seen the actual face of God.

He is one of a few who is charged with keeping the great beast in check.

The Black Knight has ridden throughout the mountains, certain that he will find The Leviathan here somewhere. As always, he has had to operate independently of the church. He can tell no one of his work, except the others who share the burden. He met up with another of his order in the mountains outside Bucharest some months ago. The beast remains a step ahead of them, everywhere they look.

He has exhausted his search around Geneva and is ready to ride out of the city.

People continue to stream into the city, looking for help. For healing. For hope.

The Black Knight has none of this to offer.

Walking with the people toward the entrance to the city is a man in a long blue cloak. He steps in the path of the horse ridden by the Black Knight.

The Knight looks down at the man in blue, who looks up with a smile.

"Leaving so soon, Sir Knight?"

The Black Knight smiles back at him. "I was unable to find that which I sought. And you?"

The man in the blue cloak raises his hands to shoulder level, and turns back and forth. "I feel that I am needed here. There is so much work to be done."

The Black Knight sits high in his saddle. "You cannot undo all of the work that lies before these people. It is the will of God that they should be made to suffer the corruption that stalks the land. Perhaps they will take a leap forward and become stronger for it."

"Perhaps," the man in the blue cloak says. "What price, though, must they pay?"

"That is not ours to decide. We can only do what we can. We all wear the chains He has placed upon us, my friend."

"This is true, Sir Knight. And to that end, I bid you safe travels. Happy hunting and all glory to God."

"Glory be to God," the Black Knight replies.

He pokes his horse in the ribs with his heavy boots and rides out of the city of Geneva.

The man in blue looks at the people around him and takes a few seconds to be bothered by the plan his God has in place for the people of the world today.

Such thoughts, though, are not in his nature. They are certainly not something he is supposed to be thinking. He decides to put it out of his mind, and see what he can do to help Geneva with the scourge that comes through the gates.

"The Korean Bodega? Seventeenth and Church?"

"That's the one."

"Man, Sang *knows* me. He knows my mother an' shit. I hit Sang's and he figure out it me...I can't *never* go home."

"You *is* home, bitch." Jay smiles, and sits forward in his immaculate red Adidas sweat suit. "You gotta make yo' bones, though, man. You hit Sang's...you one of us."

"Ain't there nobody I can take a shot at instead? I wouldn't mind some wetwork, man."

Dare laughs out loud suddenly, and several of the other West Side Kings look in his direction and laugh in kind. "You mean you ain't afraid to pop somebody's ass but you won't do a little lifting at the Bodega?"

Jay smiles wide, but he isn't laughing. "I guess Babyface more afraid of his momma than he is of murder."

The entire room laughs, including Babyface.

Jay nods at him. "You a smart young man, Babyface. I can use smart young men."

The boy exhales, as if he had not taken a breath in a week. There is still a level of tension in the room, and he can feel it is firmly as he can feel the temperature in the moist air outside.

"But you still owe me everything in the cash register at the Korean Bodega at Seventeen and Church. Take Payday with you. I'll expect you at midnight."

He holds out a six-shot pistol.

An hour later, Babyface and Payday are leaning up against the wet wall of the Brownstone next to Sang's Korean Bodega.

Both are smoking cigarettes. Payday is 19 and has smoked for six years. Babyface is 15, and he started two weeks ago. He did so because someone suggested it would make him look tougher. Overcoming a nickname like Babyface is not the easiest thing to do, especially when you really, truly have one.

A pair of customers says good night back to Sang. A pair of ski masks slides over a pair of faces. In a window, a pair of eyes belonging to a little girl observes this, and sneaks out of her bedroom.

Payday hands Babyface the gun.

"S'all you."

"Let's go," Babyface replies, but his tone is a lot shakier and more uneasy than he would like it to be.

In what would best be described as a trot...not a run, not quite a briskly paced walk...they casually and quickly push into the Bodega and brandish the gun.

Sang has been robbed before. He has run this business for many years. However, it happens infrequently and he isn't entirely sure whether the pistol under the counter is actually loaded or not.

He is certain that he isn't going to take the chance.

"Register! Now!"

The voice is familiar, but Sang says nothing. Give them what they want, they go away. You are less likely to get hurt that way. Let the security company and the insurance sort it out. He has video recording everything. At least everyone will know he did not make it up.

"S'cuse me, Mister Sang?"

The smell came through the door before the woman did. Erma Gird is standing there with The Duck Man. She is looking expectantly at Sang, not the boys. The boys are becoming increasingly annoyed by this, as they are the ones holding the gun. Generally that is the best way to be the people in a room that command the most attention.

"Hello, Erma. What can I do for you?"

"You know how you sometimes give us some of the fountain coke?"

Sang looks past The Duck Man to the Soda Fountain. The Duck Man has a patch of a duck on the grimy hat sitting smugly on his head, and a real duck named Elvis sitting out in front of the store, waiting for him. The Duck Man is saying nothing. Anyone who knows him…Sang included…usually appreciates his silence. The Duck Man tends to freak people out with his psychotic town crier routine.

Now The Duck Man is a loaded gun all his own in this situation. His strange free-flowing fake headlines could have one of two effects on these men with the actual gun…these *boys*, really. They might leave the building peacefully to get away from The Duck Man. They might become agitated, and start shooting.

Either way, Sang decides he probably should see where Erma is going with her question.

"Yes, Erma. Why?"

"A few of us were wondering if we could have some cokes tonight."

At that moment, 20 additional homeless people walk into the bodega. They stand at the register, facing the boys with the gun. They all look very, very unhappy.

One speaks, very casually, as if he does this without fear. When one has nothing to lose, one has no fear. When one has no fear, he can be relaxed in the face of death.

"You are in the wrong neighborhood, boys. This extablishment is protected by The Mayor of Seventeenth Avenue."

"You mean *establishment*, Rudy," Erma corrects. "With an 'S'"

"Whatever," Rudy says with a dismissive wave of his hand. "Anyway, you should put the gun down, son. Sang has maybe 30 bucks in that register. Nobody wants to beat the crap out of you guys for 30 bucks."

"We will, though," says a rather tall man in a thin green Army jacket. Someone else was president when he wore it for the first time. Someone else was also President the last time he shaved his face.

By way of response, Babyface cocks the gun, and opens his eyes, wide. Through the red-ringed eyeholes of the black ski mask they are as white as the cue balls on the pool tables at Honey's. It is the stare of desperation and uncertainty.

Conversely, Payday has his eyes closed now. He has tilted his head to the floor. He has been in this scenario before. He is even shaking his head and smirking under his mask. He exhales in frustration.

"We out," he says. He puts a hand on Babyface's shoulder. The boy flinches and nearly fires the gun.

"We ain't shit," he replies.

"Now there, I can agree with you," says Rudy. "You ain't shit. You're in deep shit, but you ain't shit."

"I will shoot every one of you mother…"

"No," Rudy says, smiling, "not really. At best you can shoot three of us before you ain't holding that gun no more. Four if you're really good. I'll bet you ain't. You might be lucky to get two of us. Then you become a murderer instead of a robber. You ain't no murderer, son. You just need to go now."

Babyface uses his bright white, wide eyes to

look around the room. Sang has continued to stand perfectly still, which means he still hasn't put any money in any bag. The 22 homeless people who have suddenly inserted themselves into his robbery continue to stand like Leonidas and the 300 at the Hot Gates of Thermopylae. There are no other customers in the bodega, and Payday is looking at him.

Payday is wearing a mask. Despite this, Babyface knows absolutely everything Payday is saying to him with his facial expression. It isn't a pleasant message.

Babyface realizes he has just been screwed out of his first chance to make points with the West Side Kings. Chances are pretty good he's going to get his ass beat if he goes back there. And he has to go back there and take it like a man, if he ever expects to have the chance to make a name for himself on these streets.

Babyface lowers the gun.

Rudy smiles. He says nothing, doesn't rub it in at all. There is no need. Everyone in the room knows it's over. They knew it long before Babyface lowered the gun.

Erma and The Duck Man are still in the doorway. They step to one side to let Babyface and Payday walk by as they leave without a word, heads hung low.

The urge to laugh at them is almost too much to bear, but they manage to silently maintain their victory, rather than stir up something else. Safety in numbers is one thing, but pushing it could result in dire consequences later on when they are outnumbered.

Sang takes a long, deep breath and lets it out.

"So," he says, "who wants a coke?"

The cellar is brooding and black. The thin light of the street lamp that streams through the tiny window near the ceiling is little more than a moonbeam fighting its way into a dark forest.

It knows. It is very aware that he draws near.

It smiles.

COME, OLD FRIEND.

It hears the tones of its own voice bounce lightly around the room. The fieldstone and mortar have a pleasant vibration to them.

COME AND VISIT ME AT LAST. YOU HAVE FINALLY FOUND ME AGAIN.

This Saturday Night is dark, darker than most.

The rain has let up but the skies continue to be overcast and grim. The night finds the man in black in prayer.

He sits with his legs crossed in what used to be called "Indian style" a generation before, and appeals directly to his God. He sits in Adrian's Alley. No one, not even a cat, is anywhere near him.

"Once more, Lord, I answer the call to hoist your light upon this world. Hear your servant, for I would have your attention now as I shield myself in your powerful light."

He removes an ornate, golden knife from his

long black coat and lays it in his lap with one palm on the hilt and the other on the blade.

"Our relationship has been contentious, O Lord. We have had many times where we did not see eye to eye. Your mysteries are not mine to understand, and your whims are mine to obey."

A rumble of thunder can be heard overhead, as if carrying a message of agreement from on high.

"Hear me, O Lord, as I demand the honor of carrying your favor into battle. I will defeat your enemy once more, and return to you a brilliant champion. I will redeem myself, and I will show you that my fall was something to be forgotten to the faintest ages of time."

Rain has begun to fall quite heavily. The man in black has not moved, not even flinched.

Chairman Meow has ventured to the edge of the drier spot protected by an overhang. He is looking at the man, but keeping his distance. The rain gives the cat an excuse to be uncomfortable without looking quite so uncomfortable in front of the other cats. Even in the feline world, appearance is everything.

The man in black grips the handle of the knife and holds it over his head. He is murmuring to himself. He is the only one sitting there, but there is a susurrus…a chorus of voices chanting under its breath and invoking words of power along with him. This is what Chairman Meow hears, anyway. Perhaps the rain is giving echo to his words. Perhaps the old cat's ears are playing tricks on him.

Lightning illuminates the alley. It remains empty, save for the man in black. Had someone else been in his vicinity, he would not have noticed. He is holding the knife with a purpose now and is turning his left hand over.

His palm is up and his fingers are outstretched as he slashes a red line along what a palm reader would call his Head Line. He leaves the blade sitting in his hand, and the contrast of his dark purple blood on the well-polished gold of the blade is striking in the instant before the rain washes it off.

As if a switch has been thrown somewhere, the man in black suddenly becomes very aware of the alley, the cat staring at him from a relatively dry spot in one of the back service entrances of the Adrian Hotel...and of singing. It is a very soft, sad singing, and it comes from somewhere beyond the Eighteenth Avenue side of the alley.

The voice is female and elderly by human standards. She is singing a song by Ella Fitzgerald. The man in black has heard it before. It was mournful then, and it is mournful now. He wonders who is singing it, but not enough to go and investigate its source.

He has work to do.

He turns away from the direction of the singing, and strides with great purpose and determination toward Seventeenth Avenue.

He places the gold knife back in his coat.

The rain bounces off the pavement all around him. It slams into his coat and makes an incredible amount of noise as it falls at a rate the city has not seen in some time.

It makes him almost completely invisible to the traffic cameras as he walks toward Church Street.

As he arrives, and stares up at the magnificent architecture of St. George's Catholic Church, there is a flash and a loud booming sound.

The storm has overloaded something somewhere. A power outage engulfs the entire western segment of the downtown area.

Unseen by any electronic eyes, the man in black walks through the front entrance of the church.

The church is dark. If darkness was capable of growing up afraid of the dark...*this* is the dark that could have accomplished that.

The city's blackout backup plan has not managed to restore power to roughly half of the affected grid. Everything this side of Blanche Street, which is several blocks from here, remains in the dark right now.

The only light comes from the violent thrashes of lightning that accompany the hard-falling deluge of rain. It throws interesting shadows and colors into the main sanctuary. The figure in black moves toward the apse.

He is reaching out with his mind, something he has done for millennia when trying to sense the presence of others. In this form it is yet another of the many abilities he is discovering he no longer possesses. It has been some time since he wore a human body, and already it has found a way to annoy him.

He's in the aspe's small chapel now, listening to the darkness. She's here, somewhere. He's certain of it.

The wound on his hand is itching. The knife that made the cut is becoming hot, and begins to vibrate slightly.

The man in black fails to suppress a smile that can be described only as "giddy". His breathing quickens a bit as he hears the first sounds of heavy breathing rising up around him from the vents in the floor.

Somewhere deep within the halls of the blackened church, the man in black hears the unmistakable sound of a heavy door being flung open. It echoes throughout the building.

His right hand tightens around the handle of the knife. He closes his eyes and walks back into the main sanctuary of the church.

"Now we dance."

A roar resonates within the building as a clap of thunder shakes the outside of it.

The man in black can't help but notice the hairs are beginning to rise up on the back of his neck. He isn't entirely sure what that is supposed to signify.

Saturday night gives way to Sunday morning in the city.

Wipers dance back and forth across a few windshields, their work never truly finished, droning through the gray of the city's pre-dawn. None of the people driving toward the hospital takes much notice of the old man who walks out of the Pierce Building walking the opposite way down the one-way street.

The rain has been striking the asphalt for the better part of six hours. It's a fresh coat of clear-shine applied to the blacktop streets. They stretch through the Downtown Business District under a series of green street signs and blinking lights that sway in the light wind. The rain waters the rooftop plants at St. Brigid Regional Hospital. There will be flowers, which will bring smiles to the patients and families on the top floors of the Oncology Building. Smiles for people who could truly use them.

Farther up Seventeenth, the rain tries in vain to wash away the blood and urine in the alley beside a tavern called Honey's. The best it can manage to do is slightly improve the smell of a man sleeping next to the bar's dumpster with a nearly empty bottle of gin.

It will be another couple of hours before the sun comes out, but someone is already up.

The Mayor of Seventeenth Avenue is sitting in a puddle, thinking.

In his head, the puddle music is going *tinky-tink-tink-tink*, a happy piano rag from an era he cannot possibly have lived in.

In truth, it accompanied a silent film he saw many years ago, in a comfortable private theater room, flanked by extravagantly attired debutantes. If his brain would permit it, he would remember this. However, his brain refuses. The Mayor associates the music with rain because it was raining in the movie.

He has no recollection of the man he once was. In small ways, his brain fights back here and there. The struggle continues.

The Mayor chose this spot for two reasons. Foremost is the close proximity it has to the gym. He leers at the early group of spandex-clad housewives through the windows of *Contours* because it helps him think. Second, the cool water seeps into the bottom of his thin pants, soothing his rash. The rash is an annoyance. He makes a mental note to look for some soap today when he checks the trash bins at Market Plaza.

It is very early on a Sunday morning, so cars are rare, even here in the busy part of Downtown. In another hour, people will be making their way past his seat at Seventeenth Avenue and Grove Street, to worship in the ornate stone temples of Church Street. Right now, however, the 24-hour gym is the only real center of activity.

A bread truck, en route to Market Plaza, thunders past The Mayor and splashes water just short of him. The driver did not see him, not that it likely would have mattered.

The Mayor's heart sings as the rain dances around him, soaking into the wool of his overcoat. The Mayor is happy when the fair maiden in the green leotard is at Contours. She will never know it, but she is the love of his life. It is an innocent, pure love that he would rather take to his grave than ever approach her.

She is always wearing the same green leotard and sometimes works out on back-to-back mornings. Either she has more than one of them, or she launders it when she gets home. Or she smells a lot like he does.

The first snake escapes his notice: no easy feat, as The Mayor is one of the most observant people in the city. As the second, third, and fourth slither past the recycling canisters, The Mayor rises from the puddle and secrets himself behind the light pole despite the snakes paying him no mind at all. Water rolls out of the seat of his pants, meandering down his legs as he watches two dozen snakes rolling by. They march, for lack of a better term, directly past him on the other side of the street, heading toward the Porter Building.

"What the devil...?"

Both the snakes and The Mayor of Seventeenth Avenue sneak up either side of the street. They head northeast toward Church, the major cross street that sits a block away from Contours. Dawn is starting to gain a foothold, and a thin light of sun is about to muscle in from between the skyscrapers along Sixteenth. The Mayor loves this time of the day with its eerie quiet.

He looks across and notices the snakes are not keeping up with him anymore. He doubles back, craning his neck in the rain to see them. He spots the last handful of serpents slithering into the hidden crack in the foundation of the Porter Building.

The Mayor waits another 20 minutes without

111

making a sound, listening for any evidence that someone else has spotted the reptiles.

Hearing none, he retreats to his office to record this in the official Record.

Along the way, he mutters to himself, very quietly. He speaks in low tones, repeating a coded message that will remind him of what he has just seen. The Mayor has a tendency to forget things.

This morning, as the sun struggles to break over the skyscrapers of the city, the rain is falling hard. Even without thunder, the rain is still loud enough to annoy Paper while he configures his myriad notes. The pounding of rain on the metal roof of his shed is like an ensemble of musical hammers.

Paper has his bad cough again this morning and his stub is itchy. The stub where his hand used to be always itches when the weather is like this. He tries not to think about it as he moves across the light traffic of the not-quite-breakfast-rush of a Sunday morning. He's always paying close attention, always making his rounds. He prefers to take one more stroll of his immediate territory each morning before he reports to The Mayor.

Paper covers roughly four blocks. He personally keeps a close eye on the major part of The Mayor's territory. St. Brigid Hospital and the adjacent Piedmont Street to Port Street. Port to Grove. Grove to Church. And, finally, Church to

Sawyer. He doesn't cross Sawyer.

Ever.

Sawyer has the train tracks. Paper hasn't crossed the tracks since the night of the accident, the night his mother had her breakdown. His boys always cover the territory northeast of Sawyer Street for him. No one has left him any serious notes yet this morning, including the ambitious young Zoey, whom he is considering giving the Church to Sawyer beat to. She's proven herself time and again, and Paper isn't getting any younger.

Paper coughs as he walks down the concrete steps that lead to the boiler room of the Pierce Building at Seventeenth and Grove. He finds the Mayor awake and listening to the rain.

"Good morning, Mister Mayor."

"Good morning, Paper. What does the day look like today?"

Paper leans against the cold concrete wall. The skin on his little arms forms that vacuum seal on the wall surface "Attempted robbery last night at Sang's. Thwarted by the crazies."

The Mayor grins and cocks an eyebrow at him. "*Thwarted*?"

Paper smiles. "I read the books you give me, sir. I was bound to pick up bigger words. Let's see...oh! I noticed Buzzy's got hold of a bottle, Mister Mayor. He's in the alley behind Honey's gettin' good an' hammered."

"Sit, boy," gestures The Mayor, pointing to a folding chair at the table. "Eat."

When Paper continues, he speaks with his

mouth full. The Mayor has a fondness for the little elf cookies the bodega at Port & Sixteenth throws out after the freshness date is too far gone to ignore. He also has enough fondness for Paper to share them with him. And only him.

"So, if yer still lookin' to ffettle that thing, Miffter Mayor, I'd give him another hour and he'll be..." he swallowed, "...easy greasy."

The Mayor smiles. "Thank you, Paper. But I have decreed that Buzzy shall have a pass in that matter. He is working on a different Thing now, a minor thing I need accomplished this week."

When The Mayor speaks, it is always with an air of aristocracy, a hoi polloi haughtiness that betrays the intense smell of aged filth that rolls out from his flesh, and clothing. And when he refers to important business as a Thing...you can hear him capitalize the "T".

Paper chewed. He chewed four cookies at once. The Mayor watched this for a time, fascinated. The boy was a pure spirit, and he made The Mayor smile when he was around.

"Is there anything else, my young ward?" He slid a cold glass of milk across the table. The milk was fresh because the Feinman's delivery guy brings an extra crate each Tuesday and Friday, leaving it where The Mayor's scavengers can collect it. The delivery guy was homeless here once. He remembers his good fortune every morning when the alarm goes off, and he has the chance to go to work. He once lived under The Mayor's protection.

Paper gulps half the glass at once, a

herculean effort that would choke most people. He wipes his mouth with the sleeve that covers the stump where his right hand used to be.

Every time he does that, The Mayor aches a little inside.

"The cops keep spendin' more an' more time on the corner at Sawyer." He stifled a small burp. "Not sure who they're watchin' yet, 'less they think the hoagie shop is dealin' meth again. Which they ain't."

The Mayor rests his head on the back of his hand, leaning against a steam release valve that hasn't really worked since the Clinton administration.

"Pay a call to the lads at Adrian's Alley. Inform the Jew, the Duck Man, and the Blind Arab that I wish a quorum."

Paper smiles. He isn't sure what it means, but he thinks *quorum* is a pretty neat word. He drains the glass, and The Mayor pulls two large coins out of his pocket. He pauses, and then pulls out a third. He hands them to the boy.

"You are a good and faithful knight, Paper. Go back to the women's shelter first and kiss your mother. And watch for snakes."

"Snakes?"

"Snakes."

Tilting his head like a curious terrier, the boy leaves. Once Paper has vanished back into the pipes that lead to the exit hallway, The Mayor of Seventeenth Avenue pulls a little red ledger out of his coat. He scribbles a few notes into the official Record. They are just symbols and sketches, really, something only he can decipher. Not even Paper is privy to The Mayor's system of notes.

Only three times over the years has a police officer removed The Record from his person. Three times, a frustrated man in blue who does not understand who and what the law really is on Seventeenth, has returned it.

The Mayor picks up the boy's glass, and moves back into the living area.

Father Vaughan is on his knees as the first rays of cloud-filtered sunlight lean into his huge, stone church. The rain that greeted him when he came in this morning is almost gone. The city always smells better to him after a good soaking rain.

The smell doesn't reach here though. He is wiping the last of the blood from the downstairs hallway, so the children will not encounter it on their way to Sunday school. He is thankful for small favors, thankful young Glorianna has not come in early to set up any art projects for the little ones. There would be no way to explain the mess. There is precious little time to make it go away.

St. George's sits on the corner of Church and Seventeenth. It was the first permanent house of worship built in the city shortly after its founding 130 years ago. The road to the huge building from the Old Town District...Church Street...is one of the city's original streets and became the trunk from which the tree of Downtown spread her branches.

Next to St. George's on Seventeenth Avenue is a strip mall. Until the 1930s, a railway station sat there. The diocese actually petitioned the state government in 1899 to stop trains from passing through the city on Sunday mornings because their sound and vibrations were disturbing services. They were successful. The church always has held great sway in this part of the country, no matter which particular church it was.

Father Vaughan's cassock, immaculately clean, hangs waiting for him in his office. He had to take it off when he discovered the mess, and he scrubs the floor in an old set of Boston College sweatpants and a sleeveless T-Shirt. This part of the church is always cold, and his arms are as icy as his resolve.

"No one is here yet," he says in the direction of the cellar door. He says it loudly enough to be heard beyond it. "You are usually more careful than this."

The door swings open abruptly, revealing only pitch-blackness from the creaky wooden stairs that wind down to the unused cellar. The voice that responds is equally dark, creaky, and abrupt.

I WAS WOUNDED. HE BORE AN ENCHANTED WEAPON.

Father Vaughan stops wiping to hear the next reply but does not look up. A drop of sweat lands with a *plap* into the freshly scrubbed bit of marble beneath his face.

"Are you all right?"

117

YOUR CONCERN IS MISPLACED.

Father Vaughan continues his scrubbing upon hearing this.

OF GREATER INTEREST, FATHER, IS HOW HE BROUGHT THE ENCHANTED WEAPON ALL THE WAY TO OUR DOOR.

"There were rumors that the knife had been here in the church all along."

NO, I AM CERTAIN HE BROUGHT IT WITH HIM.

"So you knew this man. You've met him before in another time and place."

I HAVE, YES.

"How did he come to find you here?"

I COULD NOT PERSUADE THAT ANSWER FROM HIM BEFORE HE DIED.

"I see."

YOU SHOULD KNOW THAT I SENSE THE PRESENCE OF YET ANOTHER WEAPON NEARBY. HE WAS ONLY THE BEGINNING. MORE LIKE HIM UNDOUBTEDLY WILL COME. THEY WILL MEET THE SAME FATE. THEY WILL NOT GET IN THE WAY OF OUR WORK.

"I agree," Father Vaughan said. He was relieved that his next question...regarding the attacker's whereabouts...was answered before it was asked. He gave the marble a final wipe down. "First we will have to identify the weapon in the lore. I assume you have it?"

I DO, THOUGH I DARE NOT TOUCH IT AGAIN. WHAT SCRUTINY I CAN GIVE IT FROM A DISTANCE SUGGESTS IT BELONGS TO ONE OF THE ELDER HUNTERS. THIS IS

WHY I AM CERTAIN THAT I HAVE ENCOUNTERED HIM BEFORE. IT IS UNLIKELY THAT HE CAME UPON THE WEAPON BY OTHER MEANS.

The Priest rose to his feet. "And he knew you were here."

HE HAS HIS METHODS. I TRUST YOU HAVE NOT RECONSIDERED YOUR END OF THE BARGAIN AND SPOKEN OF ME?"

The Priest walked the bucket with the scrub brush over to the cellar door, and set it down at the top of the steps.

"I have been given two precious gifts by Almighty God: your life and my own. I would do nothing to compromise either of them."

After a second, he added, "Partner."

CONSIDER NOW THAT OUR ENEMIES SEEM TO HAVE A FIRM IDEA OF WHERE I TAKE MY REST. WE MUST BE STRONGER IN OUR AWARENESS AND OUR RESOLVE.

"And our discretion," the priest added, dropping the sponge back into the bucket. "This cannot happen again."

OF COURSE IT CAN. ALL THINGS ARE POSSIBLE.

Father Vaughan walked down the hallway to the stairwell that led to his office's back door. As he began to climb them, the bucket was gone.

The cellar door closed itself firmly.

After a long and badly needed nap, Paper

emerges into a cloudy afternoon from the doorway of the Women's Shelter. His mother was not in the room when he woke up, and as usual, he was able to slip out before anyone from the staff could intercept him and insist that he stay until she returns. One of his many reporters, the little girl named Zoey, is at her usual post at the Korean Bodega waving him over with all the subtlety of an airport flagman. Paper crosses Church Street uneasily, still a bit lethargic as his immune system continues to battle his wee beastie infestation.

"Hi, Zo'."

"Paper, that creepy guy with the gold knife went into the St. George's last night, and he didn't come out."

Across the street, Paper sees the older kids leaving the afternoon Bible Study Group. One of them locks eyes with him as if moved to wonder why their worlds are so different. Paper, however, never wonders this.

"This is the guy that was preaching outside of Honey's Friday Night?"

Zoey toes the sidewalk. "That's him. Kept sayin' somethin' 'bout the devil's servant until The Mayor got him to leave. By that point, I heard somebody kicked him in the face."

Paper coughs. Something foul rises from his chest, and he walks around the side of the building to spit it out. It would be disrespectful to spit at the storefront.

"Thanks, Zo'. I'll go let The Mayor know. Anything else?"

"Buzzy's passed out with an empty in Adrian's."

"Yeah, I saw him this morning, before it was empty. Sad. He was doin' so good." Paper sighs, and in doing so, hears and feels more congestion.

Zoey needs something to do. "S'pose I should go over and poke him? Make sure he ain't dead?"

After walking to Adrian's with Zoey to make sure Buzzy is still breathing, Paper wanders over to the cellars of the Pierce Building. He finds The Mayor blessed with a rare visit from Chairman Meow. The cat seems especially needy for some reason, and the Mayor is holding and stroking him. Given the size of the cat, this is done with some difficulty.

"What is it, Paper?" The Mayor of Seventeenth Avenue asks this without looking up from the Market Plaza Penny Shopper laid flat on the table.

"Crazy Preacher Guy from Honey's? With the knife that looks like the one everyone was talking about?"

"Yes?"

"Went into St. George's last night and didn't come out."

The Mayor looks up and says nothing. He sets Chairman Meow onto the table, offers Paper a chair, and takes one himself.

Paper coughs and takes an elf cookie from

the package on the table and stuffs the whole thing into his mouth. He coughs again, spraying a small dusting of crumbs onto the table.

The Mayor doesn't seem to notice this. His arms are on the table, his hands together, fingers steepled, deep in thought.

"That's three then. One is strange. Two, a coincidence. Three is worth looking into."

"Yeah, but…what'f the connectfion?" Paper asks, his mouth still full, more crumbs raining down on the dirty tabletop. Chairman Meow has begun cleaning them up, as is the nature of cats. Helpful creatures, all.

The Mayor touches his steepled fingers to his dirty forehead.

"The first was Jimmy Nose. Tuesday night. Broke into St. George's. No one saw him come out, and Father Vaughan said nothing was stolen. No one is going to miss Jimmy Nose anyway. Just another would-be gangster with no brains."

"And after the break-in, my boys have been careful to keep an eye on the church. We'd've known."

"And, of course, once word gets out that the building has bad security…someone else has to try and do it better."

Paper nodded and coughed. "Enter Pete Gravy."

The Mayor rises, and begins to pace like a detective piecing it all together. "Thursday night it was Pete Gravy, noted restaurateur, wife-beater and petty thief. He breaks in using the same door. Only, when the cops arrive, there's no trace of him."

Paper is eating another elf cookie. "And now Cray-fee Preachy Guy."

The Mayor pours Paper a glass of milk. "Yes. Now, last night, Crazy Preachy Guy."

Paper drinks and wipes the milk from his mouth.

"What's a restaura...?"

"Never mind, Paper."

Paper is thinking something big is afoot that the rest of the administration of Seventeenth Avenue will want to be privy to. "So," he asks The Mayor, "Another quorum?"

The Mayor opens a door for Chairman Meow, who has been scratching to leave the room, as if they were boring him. They were. The crumbs have stopped flowing, after all.

"No. Let's leave the others out of this, until we have more answers than questions."

Adrian's Alley always remains dim in the strong light of the middle of the day.

This is because it finds itself tightly wedged between a number of tall buildings. In fact, the buildings in question are part of a block of skyscrapers, some of the biggest in this part of the country. The two towering monoliths of the HCR Towers bracket the northwest end of the alley where it meets Eighteenth Avenue. The famous Adrian Hotel, where a popular film was shot in the 1950s, sits on the other side of the alley.

Adrian's Alley then wriggles to the southeast, around the huge parking garage the city finally repaired a couple of years ago, until it finally snakes past the Porter Building at Seventeenth. The Porter is tall but less than half as tall as the HCR Center.

The alley is too narrow for any traffic other than that of the foot variety. The alley is also too close to the buildings to have much of a gang presence. All in all, Adrian's Alley is a relatively safe part of the city, which makes it a popular place for the drunks to pass out in at night.

In the many years since the alley was created by the layout of the city, there has never been a violent crime on this little strip of pavement and dirt. Not even in the late days of the nineteenth century, when many of the people in this part of the country still carried sidearms and died in their boots.

Today, though, there are no cowboys to be found here. Today, Adrian's Alley pretty much belongs to all the cats.

The Cats of Adrian's Alley are afforded a sort of respect unseen since the days of their ancient ancestors in Egypt. They run freely without fear of man. They are spoiled by all of the attention the people who walk here give them. It is lavished on them by passing children, devoted shop owners, and a loving population of homeless street people.

Legend has it Chairman Meow was once The Mayor's pet, until the old man lost his mind. This happened right around the same time the cat is said to have become *self-aware*. When you see

Chairman Meow, you are more than a little certain the cat is deciding something about you.

Chairman Meow has fathered at least half of the 30 known cats in the alley, which runs all the way up to Eighteenth Avenue behind the Porter Building and its huge neighbor, The Adrian Hotel.

Nicholas Prince is working on a Sunday, and walks past the alley with one of his grandsons. Marcus is 11 years-old and carrying a bag from Sappia's while they walk. Every dozen steps or so, his lips tighten around the straw in a cherry coke. Grandpa has root beer because Grandpa loves root beer.

When Nicholas has to put in a few hours on the weekend, he tries to plan it for Sunday around lunchtime. He and Marcus get hoagies from Sappia's and have lunch in Grove Park. He does this a few times each week, actually, but he cherishes the chance to do so with his Grandsons. Darius may not be interested anymore, but Marcus is.

They always ask for an extra slice of turkey, which Marcus wraps in a napkin. When they reach the alley, Marcus breaks it up and feeds the strips to whichever cats come closest to them on Seventeenth. Chairman Meow is typically not among them. He tends to stay hidden.

Nicholas smiles as he watches the gentle kindness with which Marcus feeds the cats.

He stares up the alley and wonders where Darius is right now.

In another part of the city, Dare is half asleep in the grubby little house with a crappy roof that serves as the main hangout for the West Side Kings. Someone in the gang owns it, but Dare isn't really sure who it is. There is always plenty of gin, there is always plenty of smoke, and there are always at least three members of the Kings around. It is incredibly rare to see fewer than three of the Kings together at any time. Even when they are on their home turf.

The Kings compete with the mafia and with a couple of other gangs that run the streets to the north or south of this part of town. For the most part…since leaving home and becoming a full-time member of the Kings a couple of years ago…Dare has worked his way into the upper tier. This effort was assisted in a very unfortunate way, when a turf war with the Mexicans up around Twenty-Third Avenue resulted in two bloody nights with a savage body count before both sides saw cooler heads prevail. Survivors like Dare who traded skin with *La Eme* became powerful young men within the organization. As did one woman who is probably tougher than half the men in the gang.

The young bucks are coming up below him in the pecking order. Not every kid is going to be as ineffective as Babyface was. Dare has to prove his worth to keep his spot.

This thing at St. George's is real. It has to be. Too many people have disappeared trying to get their hands on it for it to be nothing more than a rumor.

Dare is going to prove himself to Jay in a huge way. He's going to set himself up to be the next Jay.

He's sure of it.

Zoey can't sleep.

Zoey doesn't like to sleep. The world is just way too entertaining for her to waste time not watching it.

She's looking out of her window as night is falling and keeps seeing something in the street. At first she assumes it is her imagination. An established lack of sleep she consistently adds to gives way to mild hallucinations. From time to time they are unavoidable.

After a while she is continuing to see them run through the street under the street lights. Except they aren't really running so much as slithering.

Snakes. She's sure of it. Every 30 seconds or so, there's another one. This goes on for five minutes.

Her curious nature surrenders, and she finds herself jumping into her nice warm bed.

After a few minutes, the rain comes. She hops out and takes one more peek at the street.

No snakes.

Further up Church Street, though, she spots something else interesting.

She watches it for a while, wrapping her sleeping bag around herself. Sleep will have to wait a bit.

But it doesn't. Within 10 minutes, Zoey falls

asleep at her window.

Her mother checks on her after a while and puts her in her bed.

There is thunder in the mountains as Dare parks his Bonneville in the gravel lot at Twentieth and Sawyer. A lot of the West Side Kings park there when they drive. It is far enough away from where he is walking to and in a neighborhood where people know to leave their cars alone or face consequences.

The first flash of lightning lights up the sky as Dime hands the gun to Dare. Three of the car doors squeak open and the young men disembark. The kid called Be emerges from the passenger side back door and looks up at the sky. Be hates getting wet, but there's more to it than that. Be does not look any happier to be there than Dime does, and Dime was frowning before the first rumble of thunder from their west. Clearly, Dare is the only one who is looking forward to this.

Dare opens the trunk for a second and grabs the short tire iron out of it.

The rain is pounding down around them by the time they make it over to Church Street. Either no one else is walking on this part of downtown right now, or people are just staying away from them.

The cars that blow by them are driven by people who only seem interested in getting out of the rain. As the rain picks up even more Dare and his associates can't blame them in the least.

Dime watches Dare closely. Dare seems especially driven to their destination. Be hasn't seemed to notice this, but Dime certainly has. The closer they get to the church, the more Dime realizes he really doesn't want to be here. Something about this feels very wrong.

St. George's rises up into the rainy sky before them after they cross Eighteenth Avenue. Dare and Dime have made it all the way to the corner of the building before they realize he is no longer in step with them.

They both look back over their shoulders and stop walking.

Be is standing next to the mailboxes across the street from the Adrian Hotel. He has his hands firmly in his pockets, and his face is completely hidden by the soggy hood of his sweatshirt as it wraps around his head. He is standing perfectly still.

"Yo! You comin'?" Dare turns to face him completely as he says this.

Be shakes his head.

Dime closes his eyes and sighs. He's had the exact same thought for much of the last block, but now it's too late. The little shit beat him to it. Now he *has to* go in. He can't let Dare go in alone.

Dare doesn't shout anything else to Be, and Dime also has nothing to say over the rain. They turn and walk up to the front doors of the church. By the time they look back up toward Eighteenth, there is no sign of Be anywhere on Church Street.

The lock on the main doors of the church is

broken, and nothing has been done yet to shore up the building's defenses. Dare and Dime push the heavy doors open and step in out of the rain.

They shake off the wet for a moment and look around in the darkness as they dry their shoes on the large black rubber-lined rugs in the hall.

"All right," Dime says, "where we lookin'?"

Dare rubs his chin. "Gimme a minute."

Dime is a thief at heart, and in an instant he turns his first instinct into his first action without a thought. He busts open the poor box by the entrance and pulls all of the bills out of it. He stuffs them into his pockets without counting them. He leaves the change. Any thief worth his mettle knows that coins are too bulky and noisy.

"You finished?"

"Yeah," Dime says. "You ready?"

"Yeah. Let's go *this* way."

The church is dark and every squeak and tap of their shoes seems to echo for far longer than it possibly should as they walk around the ornate church. The beauty of its carvings and tapestries and stained glass are concealed by the darkness. Their loveliness and the talent behind the painstaking craftsmanship involved in their creation would be lost on these two anyway.

"It a knife. It should be where they keep the tools an' shit."

"You mean the tool box?"

"No, fool. The priest tools. The stuff the man holds. Crosses and sticks with smoke in 'em. Stuff like that."

"Where would they keep that?"

Dare looks in the main room of the church, dominated by a gigantic wood and brass cross. Behind the stage there are four doors.

"Prob'ly in one of those rooms. Come on."

They walk past the pews and notice the temperature drop a bit.

The room is filling both young men with an awful lot of self-doubt. The church has been here for over a hundred years. It's as if thousands of Sundays packed with millions of prayers are weighing down on them as they walk through the room.

Dare shakes it off because he has a burning determination to get the job done that he came here to do. Dime is starting to buckle under it and fill his thoughts with all of the horrible things he's done in his life.

He is realizing that there have been an awful lot of them.

They try the first side door, and find it to be locked. Dare kneels down and starts looking at the lock with his little flashlight.

"Check them other doors," he says, possibly more tersely than he intended.

Dime opens the second door and finds music stands leaning against each other. A worn out amplifier with the words Fender Champ is tucked back in the corner next to a guitar case. The third door has a tiny drum kit in it. The fourth is locked.

"They don't lock up the musical instruments, but they lock these other doors. Weird."

Dare isn't listening. He's doing everything he

knows how to do to jimmy the lock, and failing miserably.

"Man, this – "

A loud bang causes both young men to jump straight up and nearly double their heart rates. It came from one of the pews.

In an instant, Dare has the gun out and is holding it under his flashlight, like one of the agents on *Criminal Minds*.

"Who's there?" he asks, his voice a little more shaky than he wanted it to be.

Dime is slinking into the shadows as quietly as possible.

The beam of the flashlight bounces all around the room with abrupt movements. Dare is checking every corner, every nook and cranny of the grand chapel room from the stage. There is no trace of anyone or anything in the room that shouldn't be there, with the exception of them.

They sit in silence for at least 30 seconds before Dime says something.

"There ain't nobody there, man. Let's just get into these rooms and check 'em out."

"I can't get this goddamn lock."

"Don 't say goddamn in church."

Dare pauses. "You just did too, man, shut up."

They both laugh, if nervously.

Dare puts the gun away in his hoodie. "Come help me, then."

It takes a good five minutes to do it, but Dime finally gets the lock open on the first door. It is filled with robes and big fake candles and sensers and a bunch of other equipment neither of them can put a name or a purpose to.

No knife. Maybe some gold but no knife.

The lock on the fourth door is even more of a challenge than the first was. Eventually, Dare produces the tire iron and hacks away at the wood around the lock.

The door pops open after he destroys the area next to the knob. Dare pulls up the flashlight and clicks it on.

"Empty."

Dime can't stop himself from laughing out loud at his friend.

"Shut up."

A strange noise rises from the cellar. It is almost a growl, but it sounds vaguely mechanical.

Dime freezes in mid-movement, his arm dangling in the air in front of him in the darkness. "That the Furnace?"

"Shit, I don't know. Prob'ly. Let's go check it out."

"That wasn't what I meant," Dime hisses, but Dare is already on his way out of the room, looking for the hallway that would lead to the downstairs.

Another banging noise from below their feet brings the gun back out of Dare's pocket. Their footsteps in the old hallway echo without the squeaking that accompanied them earlier, the moisture long since deposited in the main chapel. Dare reaches into the other pocket and produces the flashlight again.

Facing the wall, he clicks on the light and

shouts in surprise.

On the wall is a very realistic-looking mural of a dragon. It is facing off against St. George, who wears a suit of silver armor and holds a sword with a gilded blade over his head, staring the creature down.

Dare's shout creates two reactions. It makes Dime jump almost out of his skin, and it brings a new noise.

A low, guttural noise like a laugh. It rolls up from the cellar...a taunting laugh. A laugh tinged with cruelty. A laugh that neither of the young men are particularly in the mood to hear.

"Somebody else is here, Dare."

Dare cocks the gun and makes sure the safety is off.

"Not for long."

The flashlight goes past his face for a moment. It happens far too quickly for Dime to decide if the look on Dare's face is one of anger or determination.

Either way, he would much rather be out of here.

The darkness is thick in the corridor, and they don't dare turn on the lights. There are a lot of windows but the streetlights seem muffled somehow, and the rain is coming down in sheets now. So it takes them some time to finally find the heavy wooden door that leads to the cellar. Along the way, they search a few other rooms but find nothing of substance.

"I don't hear it anymore," Dime says.

Dare has just now remembered to reset the

safety on the gun and has placed a hand on the door. He is listening closely and hearing the same nothing as Dime.

The door leads to a set of very old wooden stairs. There is no response from the light switch, so Dare turns the flashlight back on and begins descending the steps. They creak and groan under his feet. Dime steps onto the steps as well and doubles the noise.

"Shh!" Dime says suddenly when he reaches the bottom stair. He puts a hand on Dare's shoulder and points with the other. "Over there."

Dare moves the light over into the corner of the room opposite the furnace. The furnace is a huge, archaic thing that predates most of the buildings on Seventeenth Avenue. Nothing is in that corner. Above the nothing are the huge heating pipes. They reach across the ceiling after they emerge from the top of the furnace on the opposite wall, like massive horns from the head of a fossilized iron dinosaur.

They see nothing, but they can hear some kind of shuffling noise.

"You hear it?"

Dare does not hear it.

They both listen intensely and hear the sound of a light wind seem to rise up from the middle of the room. In the instant before a deep voice fills their ears, they realize it was the sound of someone inhaling.

WILLIAM SEIBERRY AND DARIUS PRINCE. YOU ARE WELCOME HERE. HAVE YOU COME TO ME SEEKING JUDGMENT AND

ATONEMENT?

Dime and Dare are already turning to bolt back up the stairs.

They do not get the chance. The air of the cellar seems to rush past them quickly, and the darkness becomes darker. The beam of the flashlight becomes diminished and a pair of strong hands that certainly do not feel human lift them into the air and pull them toward the center of the cellar.

Darius Prince feels his heart pounding, as if trying to break through the wall of his chest. William Seiberry has just pissed himself, and the ammonia smell fills the thin air of the room rather quickly.

The furnace leaps to life with a woofing sound and a smell of brimstone. Dare and Dime get a good look at the huge creature that is holding them up in the air.

It stands on two legs, though Dare does not understand how because it is low and thick at the waist. The head is like an old Chinese painting of a horse that looks more like a reptile. The eyes are yellow and complex with odd shaped pupils. The pupils in particular are burning themselves into Dare's brain because he is staring into them, and they are staring back.

IT IS NOT TOO LATE FOR YOU, DARIUS.

Dare feels the hand release him, and he is dropped unceremoniously to the floor.

WILLIAM, the creature says, though the mouth barely moves, YOU HAVE ABANDONED YOUR HUMANITY AND FACE JUDGMENT.

Dime hears Dare run to the stairs.

"Dare!?! What are you doing?" he screams after him.

Dare does not respond, but hears the last screams of his friend Dime follow him into the hall as he runs to the front of the church and flies through the front doors.

He can still hear Dime screaming in his head as he continues to run northwest on Church. He does not bother to return to his car one street over.

He just continues to run.

The afternoon is muggy as the sun fights with the clouds pregnant with rain over the city.

The purple Scion pulls into the parking area at Market Plaza with enough bass pumping out of the speakers for 12 purple Scions.

The window comes down and Jay leans out. He's wearing the black Adidas track suit today. He turns down the stereo to a reasonable level of bump.

"Yo, Paper!"

Paper strides over to the Scion with confidence. He knows who Jay is, and more importantly, Jay knows who Paper is. There is an uneasy peace between the West Side Kings and The Mayor of Seventeenth Avenue. Great pains are taken to maintain it. The recent unpleasantness at the Korean Bodega between Babyface and some of The Mayor's street people did not help matters much.

"Hi, Jay. What can I do for you today?"

"I come in peace, kid. I need to talk to The Mayor. He around?"

Paper shakes his head. "Nope. Off doin' somethin'. He didn't say what."

Jay rubs his chin with his hand and looks at Paper. He closes his eyes and smiles.

"Okay, maybe you can help me. I'll make it worth your while later."

Paper purses his lips. Jay isn't in the habit of offering favors so freely.

"I'm listening."

Jay folds his arms on the top of his driver's side door and leans out a little further.

"Two of my boys took a powder, and I wanna know where they are. You hearing anything?"

Paper takes another step toward the Scion. "I hadn't even heard you were short a couple of Kings. This just happen last night?"

"Last night, yeah."

Paper waves his hands at one of his boys across the street. The boy looks up and crosses Port Street. "Lemme shake the tree and see what falls out of it. Come back around three and I'll be right here."

By way of answering, Jay winks and points at him with that million dollar smile of his.

The window goes up in the purple Scion, as does the volume of its stereo, and Jay pulls out of the parking lot toward Piedmont Street.

The boy Paper had called over from across Port Street is called Ray. Ray is slightly younger than Paper and lives here on the street. Ray is also one of those people in the world everyone should have as a friend. He is that one person you know who will always get the job done. No matter what the job is or how much the doing of the job is going to suck. He is wearing a Superman T-Shirt and hat, which is a part of his usual armor each day when he rises up to take on the world.

"Jay's missing two soldiers, Ray. Hear anything?"

Ray smirks and shakes his head. "Nope."

Paper puts an arm around his shoulder.

"When The Mayor steps out of his meeting behind the synagogue at Harrison and Eighteenth, tell him to come home. I need a minute of his time.

"No problem," Ray says. Ray always says that. Mostly because with Ray it's always the truth.

Ray handles a lot of Paper's business on *all* of the streets northeast of the railroad tracks at Sawyer for him.

Paper rubs the stump at the end of his right arm nervously with his left hand again, disappearing in his own thoughts for a moment. He tells himself it's because the weather makes it itchy, but deep down he knows that isn't true.

He walks past the Hacienda restaurant packed with customers enjoying chips and salsa and walks casually up Seventeenth toward the Pierce Building to wait for The Mayor.

A missing pair of Kings. Yet another interesting development.

In a move somewhat out of character for him,

Paper fails to notice something as he crosses Port. A man in a blue suit, watching him intensely while pretending to read a magazine.

Dare stopped running very early this morning when he reached the old warehouse at 13th and Piedmont. That was about 12 hours ago.

The warehouse was once used by the textile mill on the northwest side of the city. The mill ended up being bought out by a bigger company three years ago and relocated to Nebraska.

The building has a drug problem now. It is a popular landing place for the city's heroin addicts and crack heads. It is the perfect place to hide in plain sight, which is precisely what Dare wants to do right now.

He knows that by now, Jay has sweated Be down and forced him to spill what happened last night. By now, Jay has to be looking for both he and Dime. He knows he is completely screwed. He was told to leave it alone, and he didn't. He didn't stay out of the church, and now Dime is dead. Even if Dime had survived, Dare would face Jay's wrath for disobeying him and breaking into the church.

What Dare is *not* sure about is what to do next.

Where does he go from here? Jay eventually will send someone to check out the warehouse, or get a tip from one of these burnouts looking to score. His life expectancy gets shorter and shorter the longer he stays here.

Dare has about 40 dollars on him, enough money to at least get out of the city. After that, maybe he can reach out to his Grandfather, and…

…no.

That won't work.

To his way of thinking, his family is not an option anymore. *That* is admitting defeat. He is not going to be doing that.

When he notices more and more of the drug addicts staring at him and muttering among themselves, he decides the time has come to move on.

Dare runs out of the warehouse as quickly as he ran into it very early this morning. The mid-afternoon sun is mostly obscured by clouds again today, but it is still very bright compared to the concealing darkness of the warehouse.

The clock in the tower at the Highland National Bank across the street alternates between *83 F* and *2:32 PM*.

At three o'clock on the nose, Jay's purple Scion rolls into the lot behind Hacienda at Market Plaza.

Paper and Ray are standing there. Jay is not happy to see only the two of them.

"Yo! Where the man at?"

Paper motions for Ray to stay where he is and approaches the SUV.

"The Mayor sends his apologies and means

no disrespect. But he knows a guy like you understands what it is to have business that has to be done. Business you just have to stay an' do until there ain't no more business to be done."

Jay follows this as best he can and nods.

"Whatever. You find anything out?"

Paper hands him a note written in the scrawl of one of his infamous informants.

Dare at 13th & Piedmont 230 went into theater.

"So my guess is he's catching a matinee or he's in the arcade."

Jay smiles. "Tell The Mayor I'm sorry I missed him I understand business, and I owe him one. Thanks, Paper. I owe you one, too."

He peels out very quickly and goes flying up Piedmont Street. The shadow of St. Brigid Regional Hospital begins to reach across the street as the rain clouds finally start to break up a little over the mountains.

Ray walks up to Paper, and looks to the west.

"I didn't think the sun was ever going to come back, did you?"

"Oh, I don't know," Paper says, realizing he's probably just signed someone's death warrant. "Sometimes things never come back."

He emphasizes the point by holding up his lack of right hand.

The movie sucks, but Dare isn't really paying attention to it anyway. He picked a chick flick, a romantic comedy. Something no one would expect

142

to find him sitting in.

He's trying to decide which direction is the best one to go in to get out of this situation. If he heads south, he will hit another city faster. He is fairly adept at fitting in on the streets. However, trying to do so while starting over from scratch is not the most appealing idea.

If he heads north, there's nothing but rednecks. The idea of being called *nigger* repeatedly doesn't appeal to him.

To the west, he has the mountains. They have far more wildlife than he is in the mood to have to deal with. Plenty of places to hide, but he lacks the knowledge to hide in the mountains effectively.

The east is flat and lifeless. It's boring as hell. It's one of the last places Jay would look for him.

A sudden burst of light in the hallway of the theater makes him look back behind him. He sees a girl walk out who has just left her seat and her friends walk through the door.

He turns back around to face the screen. He never sees the person who comes walking through the door the opposite way as it slowly swings shut.

Jay takes his time walking down the aisle. This is the last of the six rooms of the theater. Even when you are looking to kill someone…it is *always* the last possible place you have to look…

Dare's dreadlocks give him away. He is looking at the screen of his cell phone, which is dying. He sits back and crosses his arms as he looks up at the screen.

Someone sitting behind Dare leans forward

and whispers in his ear. "Bitch used to be on *Friends*, didn't she?"

Dare closes his eyes for a second and takes a deep breath. He turns his head a little.

"What up, Jay?"

"What up, Dare." It was a comment, not a question.

They say nothing for about half a minute, until Jay takes a chisel to the ice again. He leans forward and rests his arms on the back of Dare's seat.

"So, what the hell, dog? You jus' stupid? You disobey me, you lose Dime, you decide to keep the Mysterious Hardy Boys Treasure of the Scary Ass Church all to yo'self?"

Dare says nothing.

"You think I wouldn't come looking for you by the end of the morning? You a lieutenant, Dare. You got jobs to do. You got responsibilities. I know when they ain't be done."

Dare starts to think there might be another way out of this and takes a chance for the second time in 24 hours. His hope is that it will work out better than the first one did last night in the basement of the church.

"Look, Jay…it ain't be like that. I don't know where Dime went after we left the church. We didn't find shit. I overslept this morning. I'll get my ducks in a row after the movie. I ain't duckin' you."

Jay comes around and sits next to Dare, blocking the aisle.

"Bullshit. You been hidin' in the crack house

all morning, pissin' in yo' pants and freakin' out. People seen you. You expect me to believe you ain't duckin' me? That you just woke up late with a need to watch Jennifer Aniseed fall in love with some stupid white boy for the 10th movie in a row?"

"Aniston, man. And it's probably 20 movies by now. Look, Jay, I'm still your boy. I ain't duckin' shit."

"Then let's get out of here and go tell the boys. 'Cause they all callin' for yo' head."

A chill runs through Dare's body and causes the hairs to stand up on his arms.

"A'ight."

They rise together and walk down the aisle. The girl Dare saw walk through the door opens the door again when they are about six rows away. Light pours into the room, and Dare makes a rash decision.

He gives Jay a shove for all he's worth and sends him about five seats deep into the row they're next to. Jay gets one arm tangled in the retractable seat he lands in front of.

He steps out of his office and closes the locked door behind him. He's putting on a jacket. Every fiber of his being thinks this is a stupid idea in the middle of summer, but appearances are everything when you are sitting down to discuss a five-figure marketing campaign.

"Carolyn?"

"Yes, Mister Prince"

"I'm out for the rest of the afternoon."

"Your 4 o'clock at Wilhelm, yes. Good luck and see you tomorrow."

"Thanks. Stay cool. The rain looks like it's over for now."

"Take your umbrella anyway."

"Good idea. What would I do without you, Carolyn?"

"You would wither and die, Mister Prince."

He smiled at her. That woman was worth every penny he paid her, and she was the highest paid secretary in the company.

Father Vaughan inspects the broken lock on the closet door behind the pulpit and shakes his head sadly.

He walks slowly upstairs to his office and looks around. It looks completely undisturbed. The petty cash is untouched, the box still securely locked away in his desk. More importantly...his Coca-Cola memorabilia collection is completely in tact.

He takes his back entrance to the hall with the cellar door and pushes it open. Instantly, he knows something happened here last night.

"Are you well?"

I AM WELL.

Father Vaughan takes one more glance at the hall to make certain no one else is in the church and descends the creaking stairs.

"Visitors again last night?"

SO IT WOULD APPEAR. ONE OF THEM ESCAPED.

Father Vaughan's face turns ashen.

"Oh my Lord...*now* what do we do? This person could ruin everything!"

THIS PERSON CAN RUIN NOTHING, MY FRIEND. THIS PERSON IS UNSURE WHAT HE SAW. HE IS YOUNG, HE IS FOOLISH, AND HE IS FRIGHTENED. IF HE SAYS ANYTHING HE WILL NOT BE BELIEVED.

"Why are they coming here?"

IF I AM RIGHT, IT IS TWOFOLD.

Father Vaughan says nothing but finds a place to sit and stare into the face of the beast in his basement.

I BELIEVE THE KNIFE IS ATTRACTING THEM. I BELIEVE IT IS SUMMONING THOSE WHO ARE WORTHY OF PUNISHMENT.

"A Pied Piper of Hamlin made of gold?" He mostly asked the question quietly to himself.

I DO NOT KNOW OF THIS PIPER OF WHICH YOU SPEAK.

"Never mind. Is there a way to get rid of it? After all, it has the capability to do you great harm. This has already been proven in this very room."

IT HAS BEEN PROVEN SEVERAL TIMES OVER THE EONS. IT HAS YET TO RESULT IN MY DEATH.

"My worry is that the continued attempts to break into the church will eventually attract the sort of attention I can't just explain away. I don't like the idea of you being discovered before we have the opportunity to finish the work we have set out to do. We have so far to go before we are ready to leave the city. We should be more clandestine in our work."

THE MISSION IS PARAMOUNT. THE MISSION HAS MORE IMPORTANCE THAN THE LAWS OF MAN.

"The world has changed. Circumstances could arise that make it necessary for you to reveal yourself before you have the strength to do so."

I SEE.

"So, can we destroy the weapon?"

WE CAN DO BETTER THAN THAT.

Jay finally catches up with Dare around Nineteenth and Port.

Dare shot out one of the tires on the Scion when he ran through the theater parking lot. The police are responding to that when Dare is forced to turn around and take a shot at Jay.

Through little more than pure dumb luck, he actually hits him.

Jay was actually shot once before. He was hit in the leg during a disagreement at a card game with one of the mob crews a few years ago.

Right away, Jay knows that this is a completely different experience. At first he thought Dare hit him in the shoulder, but he took two steps and fell down, knowing it was actually his chest. He is bleeding hard and fast, and he can't figure out a way to make it stop.

One of the police cars that was headed toward the theater responds to the shot.

Jay is sitting at the side of the road and struggling for breath. He is holding his right hand over his left pectoral muscle and pressing. His track suit is getting wetter and wetter around the wound, but it is black, and the blood isn't immediately obvious to the officer who first approaches him.

Jay falls backward and lies on the sidewalk. He begins to twitch a little, and then goes very still as the officer reaches him.

Efforts to revive him fail. As Jay bleeds out, dark clouds draw in close over his head. They look down and prepare to cry.

At the same time, a power vacuum silently begins to form over the West Side Kings.

It makes the new thunderstorm starting to develop over the city look like a small sprinkle.

The Mayor is frantic at the lobby of the Pierce Building.

Many people who work in the building are always a little uncomfortable about having the strange homeless man who calls himself The Mayor of Seventeenth Avenue living in the boiler room. This is despite years of The Mayor going to great lengths to not make a nuisance of himself. The security people at the lobby level have contacted the building manager, Mr. Brandt, to come and deal with the situation.

The Mayor is in the security office. He has a stern look on his face with a trace of desperation in it.

"I need the Proud Prince, Mr. Brandt, and I need him now! No one will let me upstairs to Proud Marketing."

"What's going on Mister Mayor?" As he says this, the security guard rolls his eyes at the encouragement of this absurdity.

The Mayor leans over and puts his face in his hands.

"His grandson just shot someone and is holed up in an apartment building just a few blocks from here. The police have him surrounded."

Brandt grabs The Mayor's arm. "Come on."

They run into the lobby to the service elevator. Brandt pushes the up arrow button with a fat finger, and they wait a moment for the doors to open.

They say nothing.

A moment later, the doors open up to reveal the glass entrance doors of the Proud Marketing Group. The receptionist is taken aback when she sees The Mayor, but Brandt steps right up and quickly diverts her attention.

"I need Nicholas Prince. Now."

"Mister Prince is out," says a woman getting a cup of coffee at a neighboring hallway. "He has a meeting out of the building. I'm Carolyn. Can I help you?"

Dare isn't sure how long he's going to be able to pull this off.

The police have begun evacuating the lower levels of the apartment building. He was fortunate enough to find an apartment that had no one home when he set up a nest. It appears that no one was exactly certain which apartment he was hiding in, which finally has made it easier for him to manage a change of clothes.

There is a knock at the door.

Dare opens the door casually, as if he lives there.

"Yes?"

"Sir, I'm Officer Natarella."

"Hello, Officer Natarella. What can I do for you?"

He holds the gun handle but does not have his finger near the trigger. The barrel of the gun is in the waistband of his jeans. He is wearing a football jersey he found in the closet.

"We need to evacuate the building, sir. Please follow the fire route. Hopefully we'll have this sorted very quickly."

"Yes sir," he says, and he closes the door behind him after grabbing a winter coat on the hook beside the door. He zips it up and makes sure the back of the coat is covering his waist in the back.

Dare slips out into the hall with the rest of the occupants. None of them give him a look, and he goes out of his way to bring up the rear.

All it will take is for the police to check IDs, though, and his plan will collapse. And if they search him, they will find the gun in his waistband.

"Sir?" asks the cop, as if reading Dare's mind.

"Yes?"

"Which apartment is yours?" The officer has a clipboard.

Dare realizes that he never looked at the number on the door.

He breaks into a dead run and slips around the corner of the building before anyone has a chance to take a shot at him, though he hears several men and women yell at him to freeze. Others, likely the tenants, shout various messages about him not being one of them.

He is just entering the Eighteenth Street side of Grove Park when he hears the fastest of the police starting to close the gap between them.

Dare whips between the thicker part of the woods, moving between the trunks of the trees as the rain starts to come down again on the park.

Six officers are walking through Grove Park now, moving bystanders out of the area as quickly as possible while watching for the suspect. The kids in the skate park, including several friends of Marcus Prince, are among the first to leave the area. Marcus is not among them today. He's growing tired of having his summer trips to the park with his board interrupted by rainy days.

Dare gets closer and closer to Seventeenth. Soon, he sees no other people in the park. The police must have it pretty well cleaned out by now. Probably surrounded, too.

Shit.

Dare breaks into a dead run and emerges from the trees into a bank of blaring lights and at least a dozen police officers and cars.

"Stop, kid!"

"Don't do it!"

"Get your hands up!"

"It ain't worth it, kid…just stop running!"

"Give us the gun!"

Dare decides to give up. He reaches behind him to pull the gun out of his waistband again.

In the split second he has after the shots ring out, it occurs to Darius Prince that he probably should have told the police what he was doing.

The first officer to reach him puts a hand on his shoulder.

"Hang on, kid."

"Dragon," Dare says.

"What?"

"Dragon…in the darkness…"

Dare says nothing more as he closes his eyes and slips away.

The rain picks up and begins to wash his blood from the sidewalk in front of the bench opposite the Pierce Building.

Nicholas Prince, "The Proud Prince", as The Mayor called him, feels no pride at this moment.

He finishes his business with the police and walks alone to the parking garage where his car is waiting.

He starts the car and the stereo fills the car with music. He turns off the radio. There isn't any music in his heart this evening.

He drives around St. Brigid Regional Hospital and heads south for 10 minutes. He breaks away from the highway at that point, spends a couple of minutes on First Avenue heading toward the mountains, and turns up a few side streets.

Finally, his wheels roll onto Blue Jay Way, and he pulls his car into the driveway at the house with 575 on the mailbox.

His neighbor Jillian has been sitting on his porch with a book. She hops up when Nicholas steps out of his vehicle and starts to walk up the little path of flagstones. He buried them in the yard to create a sidewalk of sorts eight years ago, with the help of his grandsons.

"Tim and the boys are in with him. He still doesn't know."

She puts a hand on his shoulder and makes an attempt at a concerned smile.

"Anything you need, Nick," she says. The Princes have lived next door for 10 years, since he gained control of his grandsons. Tim and Jillian were there when Darius ran away to join the gang. It isn't so much a neighborly friendship as it is a bit of extended family between them. Nicholas called them to keep an eye on Marcus until he could finish what he had to take care of, and to keep him away from the news. The latter isn't particularly difficult to do, as very few 13 year-olds ever have any interest in sitting through a newscast.

"Thanks," he says.

He takes a deep breath and steels his nerve before pushing the door open.

Marcus and his friends from next door are playing hockey on the X-Box. Since no one can agree which of them can play the local team, none of the three ever do when they are together. Marcus is beating the other two, as usual.

Tim is sitting behind them on the couch, watching. As Nicholas walks into the house, he rises and meets him in the kitchen, pulling the door closed.

"Thank you," Nicholas says.

"He doesn't know anything. Should we let them finish the game?"

"I think so," Nicholas says.

"Boys…when you finish up, we're heading home."

"Okay," Luke and Cody say in unison.

Nicholas sits at his kitchen table and tries to figure out how he is going to say this to his grandson.

Tim pours him a glass of water and puts a hand on his shoulder.

The room is silent for a moment.

Jillian walks in and sits next to him at the table. She says nothing. She just wants him to be aware that he isn't alone in the room.

Nicholas Prince fights back his tears. It will only make things harder for Marcus if he's already crying.

Five minutes pass, and the Riddick family heads back across the street.

One minute after that, Marcus Prince is screaming.

Another time. Another place.

The wind whips the sand into their faces like tiny darts. It pushes itself through the thin cloth that protects their faces, and it finds its way into each and every pore. It builds up at the corners of their eyes, their nostrils, their mouths. The sand is everything and it is everywhere.

The King has demanded that they make this journey across the desert to find the one he calls The Devourer. It is said to be a demon, hidden in a cave not far from Engedi on the shores of the Sea of Lot. Messengers and vassals have been dispatched to see what the creature wants, to see if they can at least encourage it to leave this place. None have returned.

This party has been tasked with ending The Devourer and casting it back to the fires from whence it came. The time for diplomacy has come to an end. The time has come for action.

The greatest warriors in the Kingdom are making this journey. None have been left behind to defend the city behind the walls.

A neighboring City-State, a bitter rival conquered a century ago, has noticed this. Already a scout on horseback is crossing the plains to inform his Queen of the situation. The Queen is ready to take full advantage of it, and avenge her ancestors. By the end of the season, there will be no home for these sand-carved warriors to return to. Assuming any of them should survive. Their King has sent them on a fool's errand, and signed the order to put his entire Kingdom to the sword at the same time. The Devourer will destroy their Kingdom from a distance of many leagues, without picking up a single stone or a piece of steel. The City-State of Nej'iah will be lost to history. Given time, the desert will employ her ever-flowing ocean of sand to the task of erasing them from the Earth. The desert swallows memories, and forever burying the bones of entire civilizations, with a little help from the fury of the winds.

None of these brave fighters who stare down the dust storm, however, are aware of what fate has in store for their people. Right now they know only what is before them.

They know only the spreading of the warm sand beneath their sandals. They know only the sting of the sandstorm. They know only the fear in their own hearts as they force each leg in front of the other, over and over again, slowly working their way across the desert.

It should be the height of day right now, but none of them can know for certain. The skies are painted a deep, rich brown and have turned the horizon as dark as pitch. The haboob has brought night to day.

Usually, one can tell The Sea of Lot is nearby from the smell of the air. Something different within it greets you the closer you come to the edge of the water. On this day, however; they will be upon it before they see it, unless they stop and set up camp now.

The storm came upon them very quickly in the early morning, deceptive and delaying the first light of day. Now, as the day continues to drag them deeper into more and more intense sand, it has become obvious that they will have to try to find some kind of shelter.

Obvious, at least to the alchemist. He has pushed his way to the leader of the party, the Warrior known as Het.

"Het!" he shouts, fighting to be heard over the whistle of the wind and the sand. The two elements roll together into a sickly song, the music of ghosts and death filling the air all around them. "We must stop and find shelter! Men are dying back there!"

"Men will always die, Yadi" Het says, unmoved by the urgency in the alchemist's voice. "We will go forward."

Het lowers the cloth that has been covering his bearded mouth and smiles a row of stained teeth at him. "You are a man of magic, Yadi. I am a man of strength. The worlds of strength and magic hardly ever see the same thing in the same way. So it is at home, and so it is here and now in the wind and sand."

Het wipes the sand from around his own mouth.

"These men will survive."

Yadi closes his eyes for a moment before he

responds to this. "You are wise indeed, Great Het, to know the strength of a man more deeply that I. However, I know that which lies beneath the strength. And I tell you now, these men will fall before we reach the cave we seek."

Het replies with stony silence and pulls the protective curtain back over his face. He holds his cloak before him and walks into the wind.

Yadi coughs black dust and forces himself to smile. His role here is to act as the eyes and ears of his King. The King knows of Het's ambitions for his throne. The King would know how Het does with this task.

Het picks up his pace, silently daring his men to match it. They do so. It is expected of them.

Yadi does not know what drives Het to march these men through such misery, but he too must do as he is told. He quickens his own pace to keep up, wondering how many of the 100 that first set out from Nej'iah still remain.

The warriors in the Kingdom are the dominant figures. His role is speculative, supportive. Het's role is to be the thrusting forearm of his King. Mind yields to iron.

True night falls upon them, although it is difficult for them to see much of a difference. Het allows the men to rest in the diminishing wind and set up camp. He only does so because he is hungry, and he will need his men to be strong.

He continues to stare in the direction of the Sea of Lot.

HET, IN THE NAME OF JEHOVAH, I SUMMON THEE.

Het hangs his head, reverently.

THE WICKED SHALL BE PUNISHED. YOU MUST TRUST YOUR VISIONS. YOU MUST COME TO ME.

It still seems to him that no one else can hear the voice, despite the way it transcends even the winds.

Het looks back at Yadi. Even now, he has a vision of the man poisoning his own mentor, so many years ago. Yadi is a murderer hidden in the body of a weak man.

THE WICKED SHALL BE PUNISHED IN THE NAME OF JEHOVAH.

"In the name of Jehovah," he mutters. Only the wind seems to hear him.

It is heavier than Marcus expected it to be.

The weight in his hand surprises him, and a small part of his mind wonders how difficult it will be to squeeze the trigger when the time comes.

Getting the gun was difficult. His grandfather has always kept a pistol in the house. He has been a target shooter since he was in the Boy Scouts. The rifles in the gun cabinet, of which there were two, are large and intimidating to Marcus, who has never had a lesson. The pistol though...it was small and inviting. Once he managed to get the key to open the lock on the gun cabinet, the handgun and its ammunition were sitting right there for the taking.

His grandfather is exhausted. He has spent the last few days dealing with arrangements and legal paperwork and relatives. The physical and emotional tolls have been great and The Proud Prince has finally fallen into a hard sleep in the den. It is the kind of deep sleep that he so desperately needs.

Marcus walks up the street after having snuck out of the back door of his home, so as not to attract the attention of the Riddick family. He sits at the thickly painted bench of the bus stop and waits for the next shuttle to downtown.

His hand fingers the barrel of the gun in his jacket pocket.

He thinks to himself how this is going to go. The gun is fully loaded, and he has additional rounds in his zipped pocket, so he won't lose them, and he can keep shooting if he must to make good his escape. He is going to shoot the first West Side King he sees. He hopes he has to shoot more than one of them to be able to get out of there.

They ruined his brother's life. It may have been the police who actually shot Darius...but the Kings are to blame.

The Kings are going to find out how Dare's little brother feels about that.

After only a few seconds, he is joined by an old man in a blue trench coat. He sits on the opposite end of the bench and lays a blue and white umbrella over his knees.

"Nice night," he says.

Marcus says nothing.

The man in blue is looking up at the sky,

shielding his eyes from the streetlight. A few stars are visible but the clouds continue to dominate the sky, as they have for a little over a week.

"I think it will rain again though, personally. You can smell it on the wind."

Marcus shrugs.

"I have a love-hate relationship with the rain, you know," he says.

Marcus closes his eyes for a second. He has to make this bus. He has no choice but to sit here now. The man continues his new train of thought.

"I do, yes. I've lived through three floods in my life. Three. Three times I've lost everything I had, everything I held dear, to a torrent of rushing water that swept into my life with the falling rain."

Marcus makes the decision to join the conversation. Doing otherwise won't accomplish anything but could make the ride itself awkward, since the old man is waiting for the same bus.

"You in Katrina?"

The man in blue turns to face him a bit. "No. Different storms in different parts of the world. My work takes me everywhere. It has for years."

"Your work? What do you do?"

"I'm in…medicine," the man in blue says with a smile.

"A doctor?"

"Not exactly."

"Oh. Oh-kay." Marcus decides to leave that alone.

"I have every right to hate the rain, which three times has taken my entire world away from me. Instead I search for the beauty to be found in it. For me, the trick to coping with the rain is appreciating the little things."

"The little things," Marcus repeats.

"Exactly. The smell of impending rain is intoxicating, don't you think? It runs ahead of the storm, like the horses pulling a stout chariot across the dusty plains."

The look on Marcus' face suggests he isn't following him. *Know your audience,* the man in blue reminds himself, and tries again.

"Or like the offensive line paving the way for the halfback. That smell always sets the stage for the really violent storms. I know you've noticed it."

"I guess," Marcus says. He looks in the direction the bus will come from, then behind him down the glowing streetlights of Blue Jay Way. There is nothing remarkable in either direction.

He does, however, notice the smell of rain on the breeze that is coming down from the mountains. It's a little cooler than the air was this afternoon when he went for a walk and decided what he was going to do tonight. He's glad he needed the jacket to help him conceal his grandfather's pistol.

"Also, I love how quiet it is right before the rain starts to fall."

Marcus closes his eyes again and sighs with his mouth closed so as not to be rude.

The man in blue turns his body and faces forward again. "It is the same with anything, really. There is always a silver lining if you look hard enough."

"Really?" Marcus says, his word poisoned with a lethal dose of sarcasm. *"Everything* has a silver lining if you look hard enough?"

The nerve struck and exposed, the man in the blue trench coat turns again to face the teenager. There is a calmness in the man's eyes that unnerves Marcus as he speaks. The eyes of the man are very calming, and Marcus has no interest in being calm right now.

"Consider the story of the Two Brothers of Mombasa."

"I don't know that I've ever heard of the Two Brothers of Mombasa."

The eldest brother, Tano, was seduced by a world of violence and anger. He became quite powerful very quickly. Wine, women, and song were his to enjoy at his leisure. And he did. He also had what he thought to be the respect of all the people who had known and loved him his entire life. What he actually had was their fear, and the shame of having thrown that life to the dogs."

Marcus crosses his arms. The man in blue knows he has his rapt attention.

"Duma was the younger brother. He had grown up idolizing his brother, who was about 10 years older than he. Tano helped shape Duma's life, and then suddenly he was gone. He chose a new life for himself and broke the hearts of his family."

Marcus says nothing.

"One day," the man continues, "Tano

quarreled with the warlord to whom he had pledged his loyalty. The argument was over nothing of consequence, just a foolish reason to push each other to such lofty heights of anger. They drew their blades against one another and fought. When it was over, the warlord stood over the body of Tano and watched it breathe for the last time."

Marcus leaned his head back and looked straight ahead, remaining silent.

"When he learned what happened to his brother, Duma took up the sword of their ailing father and burst from their home. He searched everywhere for the warlord."

The man in blue rises from the bench, and walks over to face Marcus for the remainder of his tale.

"Alone with his thoughts as his search for the warlord continues, Duma begins to view his own anger from a fresh perspective. He tries to look at it from the point of view of what drove Tano into a life of chaos and aggression before his premature death. With his hands firmly grasping the hilt of the blade of his ancestors, Duma realized he was about to walk the same path that claimed the life of his brother."

Marcus adjusts his hands around the gun in his jacket pocket and looks down with a frown painted on his face.

"What did Duma do?"

"He returned home. He felt the pain of losing his brother for the rest of his life, but he learned to live with it. First, though, Duma knew he would have to live with himself. The thought of his father losing both of his sons to the madness of the warlord filled him with a shame far more powerful than the sorrow he felt over the loss of Tano."

Marcus shakes his head quickly.

"Duma grew up to be a great man. He learned the ways of the medicine man and saved many lives. He lived a life to honor the memory of Tano instead of throwing away his own to avenge him."

Marcus says nothing.

"But it is only an old story. I apologize. I suppose the old stories get me worked up more than they should."

The rain starts.

"Ah. And here is the rain, boy. Look on the bright side…it brings an end to my story."

The 8104 bus comes into view down the edge of the road. It has one stop to make before it will pull up to them. Marcus rises to his feet.

The man in blue hands Marcus his umbrella. "May your walk be pleasant, boy. May great things await you at the end of it."

Marcus takes the umbrella without a word and opens it. He turns and walks toward Blue Jay Way. He does not look back at the bus stop as he walks, but had he done so he would have found it empty. As soon as Marcus was a handful of steps away from him, the man in blue simply wasn't there anymore.

The 8104 pulls up to the bus stop and finds it empty. *A trick of the light,* thought the driver, who had thought she spotted a couple of people when she had crested the hill. Obviously she had been mistaken.

Per regulation, the driver comes to a complete stop at the bench anyway. She opens the door, waits five seconds before closing it again, and continues on toward downtown.

The rain continues to fall on the city's west side. The long wipers sweep back and forth on the tall windshield of the 8104.

Marcus sneaks back into his house through the backdoor. He spends 10 full minutes unloading the gun and carefully replacing each round of ammunition into the spaces in the box.

He locks the cabinet, returns the key to its hiding place under the ceramic moose on the shelf, and goes to bed.

The Mayor goes to bed that night and falls into a fitful, unhappy slumber.

Around three in the morning, a blue light fills the room, and a conversation begins that The Mayor will have no recollection of when he wakes up.

In a dream, the Mayor stands in the rain in front of the Pierce Building. He watches The Proud Prince kneel on the wet pavement across the street in an expensive suit. The man pours his heart out over the body of his grandson. It breaks The Mayor's heart to see it again. It literally gives him a pain in his chest and an empty feeling in the pit of his stomach the likes of which he has not felt in many years.

The Mayor is fingering something in his right hand. He pulls it up to look at it.

It is a wrinkled old paperback copy of *Frankenstein* by Mary Shelley. He puts it in the pocket of his grubby coat.

More than anything, he wants to walk across the street and comfort his friend The Proud Prince. He wants to offer a shoulder to the man, let him know that he is hurting as well. However, he knows that doing so is only going to put him directly in the way of what The Proud Prince has to be doing right now.

On the periphery of the scene he spots Paper, Ray, and Zoey watching everything that's going on. Keeping an eye on how the usual cast of characters around the park is reacting to it. Including remove himself on the other side of the street, in front of the Pierce Building on a sidewalk choked with looky lous.

The Mayor stands away from the throng, as he usually does. He tends to unnerve the business people and earlier in the day he burst into their lobby loudly shouting about needing to see the Proud Prince. Discretion from a distance seems to be the order of the evening for him.

A man in a blue suit and tie walks over to The Mayor. He opens a blue and white umbrella and holds it in such a way that it shields both of them from the falling rain.

The entire scene is tinged with white, and The Mayor isn't sure why. It's probably just a dream thing.

"It's probably just a dream thing," the man in the blue suit says to him.

"I was just thinking that," The Mayor says.

"I know," he says. He gestures to The Proud Prince. "Nicholas is going to be fine, you know."

"I know. But he doesn't deserve something so horrible."

"He lost his son some years ago. He mourned and then he picked himself up to take care of those boys, Mayor. He will do so again."

"Yes, he will. He shouldn't have to."

"Indeed. I will not insult the moment with any platitudes."

"Thank you."

They stand together for a moment. They watch Nicholas Prince and the President of Proud Marketing talk together as the police finish combing the place where Darius fell. The man in blue finally breaks the silence between them.

"Death has visited your street quite often in recent days. Far too often, you have to admit."

"Agreed."

"One of the deaths has affected me as well."

The Mayor looks at the man in blue for the first time and ponders this new information. He arrives at only one conclusion.

"The preacher? The man from the other night in front of Honey's? He was your friend?"

"He was. We have worked together for a very long time."

"I am sorry for your loss then. He seemed a bit...unhinged to me when we spoke."

"The man in black was a good man. He seemed to take his work a bit more seriously this time, until it consumed him. Again, I have known him for a long time, and he has waited for an age to have the chance to take up the fight again. His failure is a complete surprise to me."

The Mayor continues to stare across the street at his friend. "What fight? Take up the fight?"

The man in blue hands him the umbrella and steps out from under it. "You will learn of it soon enough. You will know what to do."

He begins to walk away, and turns his head back to add one more comment. As he says it, in reality, the man in blue is standing in the boiler room now, watching The Mayor sleep.

"And I have summoned another man in black to help you."

The light, and the man, disappear from the room.

Churchgoers are starting to trickle into the houses of worship that line Church Street when city bus 8117 makes the first downtown stop of the morning shift. Only one person steps off at the corner of Church and Seventeenth.

The Duck Man is the only one to notice the figure in black as the bus pulls away. He had been reading a soiled newspaper that reeks of fish and chips from O'Riordan's on Fifteenth Avenue. The day the newspaper is used to wrap the fish and chips, it smells fantastic. A couple of days later, as is the case this morning, the discarded newspaper smells very different. As always, the duck he calls Elvis is sitting beside him, still sleeping. Still dreaming of ponds and plump female ducks.

Operating independent of Paper, The Duck Man fancies himself something of a town crier. Unfortunately, the headlines he shares with anyone in earshot after he reads the discarded newspapers have little to do with anything printed on the pages.

"Paris Hilton is building low cost housing on the Moon! 8-Tracks are making a comeback! Cubs win!"

None of these are accurate this morning. The Cubs didn't even play.

Here's the news.

The figure in black who just got off bus 8117 is going to change the lives of everyone who encounters him in the next 48 hours.

This includes Paper, who has just arrived at the Women's Shelter, half a block to the Southeast on Church Street. His mother has given him an elixir for his cough, to do battle with his fever as well, and tucked him into her bed. She doesn't see him very often, so she clings to every opportunity that comes when she's lucid enough to mother him.

None of Paper's little network of spies, who always step up when he is out of commission, happen to be around. Only The Duck Man sees the man in black step across the sidewalk, correcting a limp with a black, silver-tipped cane. It is heavily lacquered, shining in the dim morning light like obsidian on charcoal. The grain of its wood seems impossibly deep and shiny.

Aside from the cane and the confident swagger with which he carries himself on an unfamiliar dark street...he is unremarkable. The Duck Man will not remember him.

Under his pants leg, the reason for his limp grows stronger: a renewed fire is flaring across his thigh along a very old wound. His eyebrows drop a bit, and he tucks his bottom lip in, trying to ignore the stab of pain.

He stops, and spins to face St. George's Church.

His hand tightens on the handle of his cane, and he smiles, listening.

He strolls toward Grove Street, passing the Porter Building and Adrian's Alley. Aside from a man called Buzzy, who again lies wrapped around an empty bottle of Beefeater's Gin, only Chairman Meow and friends and family are stirring there.

Chairman Meow pokes his nose out of the recyclable bins behind the Adrian to see whom these new footsteps and cane-slap belong to.

When the man in black passes Adrian's Alley, the usual cat-song ceases. Even Chairman Meow retreats, a little uneasy, toppling one of the large green containers onto the pavement. It makes a deafening noise in the heavy silence, but doesn't stir Buzzy from his sleep.

Each cat feels his or her tiny heart beat faster, until the man in black is gone and they feel the lifting of an unusual and inexplicable weight. For some of them, it is the first true taste of fear, however fleeting.

The man in black draws in a deep breath. His chest is broad and powerful, seeming to inflate a bit farther than a man's chest should, as he tastes the early morning air.

He exhales, and a thin mist escapes from his lips. The air is warm, so it is not a matter of visible breath. This is a small, purple fog. It moves with purpose, almost sentient in the way it flows. Like a river of tiny insects, or a mist of lively smoke.

It floats up, as if trying to gain a better view of Seventeenth Avenue. Then it quickly drifts behind him, into the cellar entrance of the Porter Building.

He turns around, smiling.

"Right across the road, eh? Bold."

The voice is deep. Any casual passerby who might have heard it would have been made uncomfortable by it.

He looks up at the 30 floors of the Porter, reaching into the dim light of early day. He pulls a thin cigar from his coat and puts it up to his lips for a taste.

Somehow, on the way to his mouth, the cigar has become lit during its journey.

He casually strolls past the alley again. Again, the cats fall silent.

"Watch. They'll start hasslin' the Sisters as soon as they come out of the Church. Bastards."

The shorter of the two men pulls on his hip

flask again and wipes the residue from the front of his lips before responding.

"I ain't Catholic. What do I care?" When he says the word "Catholic," it has three very distinct syllables, including a long "oh".

The taller man smacks him on the back of his head, causing him to drop the flask. It bounces on the pavement, skittering like an empty beer can over to the newspaper machine outside the Bodega.

"Ow! Hey!"

Across the street, three young men in jerseys from the city's basketball and football teams start bothering the Nuns, as predicted.

"Them are the Brides of Christ, Eddie. Them little punks should have some goddamn respect, is all I'm sayin'."

Eddie ponders this.

"And how respectful is it gonna be when we rob the church tonight?"

The Nuns make it through the gauntlet of teenagers, who continue to hoot at them, laughing.

"Useless little bastards," Mouse says, turning to Eddie. "and *that's different*. We ain't stealin' from the church. We're stealin' something that don't belong to the church."

"An' you're *sure* it's still in there?"

"Please, Eddie. Cops find somethin' that sweet, word woulda got around."

The tall one's name is Vincent, but the neighborhood and its many Police Officers know him as Mouse. He rubs his little friend on the back of the head. "Trust me, Eddie. We get that knife

174

for Paulie, and we square our debt. You know how he loves his knives. We ain't touchin' *anything* else. Pure an' simple."

"If it didn't leave the church, an' the cops ain't got it…how do *you* know where it's gonna be?"

Mouse looks around. "I'll tell you when we get in there tonight. Just be back here at nine, okay? And don't tell anyone where you're goin' or what you're doin'. I don't need your idiot brother-in-law tryin' to horn in on this. I ain't squaring his debt. Sucker bets the Pirates all the time, and can't pick a pony worth a bottle o' Elmer's glue."

Zoey, leaning against the wall around the corner of the bodega, quietly runs to the parking lot behind the building, and wanders off to find Paper.

Kitty-corner from the Bodega, in the basement of the Porter Building, there is activity. A huge, wriggling pile of at least one hundred large snakes continues to writhe around the sleeping form of the man in black.

He lays perfectly still, his cane clutched to his chest, a smile on his lips.

"What is your name, boy?"

"They call me Paper."

"Paper. That's an unusual name."

Paper rubs the stump of his wrist with his good hand.

"A name is just a name, mister. Your name

isn't who you are or what you are. It's just what people call you. And people call me 'Paper'."

The man smiles. "You have formidable wisdom for someone so young."

"I suppose."

"What does your mother call you?"

Paper looks away, and says nothing. The man in black decides not to press the issue.

"Right. Well, Paper. What can you tell me about the strange occurrences on Seventeenth Avenue?"

Paper scratches at a scab on the back of his head. "Oh, there's a lot I could tell you, mister. The question is whether or not I *will*."

Zoey spent the rest of the afternoon and evening trying to find Paper to no avail. She is beginning to form the opinion that the males of the species are unreliable. Especially since all the criminals she keeps tabs on in the course of a day are men. This can't be a coincidence.

She eats a bag of stale cheese puffs from a dusty bag, spreading cheddar cheesy spore on her post-it notes as she writes.

Her notes on the break-in, written in very pretty penmanship, are as follows:

9:10 Father Vaughan walked out of St. George's. Mouse & Eddie watched his Corolla leave.

9:20 Mouse & Eddie crossed the street and went in through the busted door.

9:30 Started looking for you or Mister Mayor. Can't find you. No cops, neither. Not even Rentacops.

9:35 Father Vaughan came back, and I dropped this note for you.

And when she dropped the note at the usual spot behind First Methodist...she also found the one she'd left for Paper earlier.

Where was he?

With more than a little uncertainty, Zoey will run up the street to find The Mayor.

But that hasn't happened yet.

At the moment, Zoey is still writing it all down on her little pad of sticky notes.

Across the street from the Bodega, where she is well-hidden in the shadows, two men are moving cautiously through the darkened church.

"What time is it?" Eddie whispers, as they step onto the stairwell.

"Why? You got someplace else to be? It's 9:20. Shut up."

Eddie looks around the building, which throws formidable shadows in the hallways. Some from the moonlight, some from the red glow cast by the EXIT signs.

"Where do we start lookin'?"

Mouse smiles, although Eddie can't see it in the dark.

"The same place we finish lookin'. Follow me."

At the end of the upper hallway, on the left, is the Priest's Office. The door is locked, but Eddie...for all his shortcomings...is a prince among lock-picks.

The door swings open with a creak that masks the sound of the outer door opening again downstairs.

Father Vaughan's office is neat and tidy, with a desktop computer and a huge reference Bible to one side. On a cabinet and two shelves behind his desk, beside the window that looks out onto Church Street and the Porter Building, are a large collection of vintage Coca-Cola Bottles and other memorabilia. Father Vaughan has cultivated this collection for many years. There are old cans and toys. There are green glass bottles written in different languages, many with different Olympic Symbols, fat Santas, and polar bears skating with penguins. A Norman Rockwell print of children drinking Cokes with their feet and fishing lines hanging off a wooden dock decorates the wall on the other side of the window.

The desk is locked. A brass letter opener with a Latin inscription on it, beside the lamp, fixes that.

Mouse regards Eddie with a raised eyebrow, as he pulls the drawer open.

"Think about it. When we was kids, and something was taken away from us in Sunday School…where did it end up?"

Eddie smiles. "Everything got locked in the desk. Genius, Mouse. Genius."

There is an ornate knife in the drawer, which looks like something out of *Arabian Nights*. Mouse pulls it out with a smile. It has jewels in the hilt, a golden blade, and seems to vibrate with a strange internal energy. There is even a faint glow, as if it is working to wrench any available light from the room, and soak it up like a sponge.

"Wow. That's it?"

"That's it, Eddie. That's what the fella was talkin' about."

"Beautiful."

Mouse returns the Priest's letter opener to the exact spot it was in before and closes the desk drawer. They disturb nothing else in the room.

"We're outta here."

They step into the main hall, pulling the door shut behind them with a click. Mouse sees the top of Father Vaughan's head rounding the top of the stairs.

Without saying a word, he yanks Eddie by the shirt to the edge of a thick, red drapery that hangs near the corner by the door, and they duck behind it.

Still as they can be, hardly breathing, they listen as the Priest's footfalls come to a stop not far from them. A hand sorts the keys on a ring, and the office door unlocks with a click.

"Come in, my children. Let's talk." The Priest opens the door all the way and enters, kicking the doorstop down to keep it open.

Mouse bangs his head softly against the cold wall behind him, looking up to the sky, sighing. He gives Eddie a shove, and they emerge from the drapery.

Together, they walk into the office.

The Priest is already sitting at his desk, not even bothering to look up. He reaches down into a mini-fridge, and pulls half a six-pack of Coke cans out by one of the empty plastic rings. He pulls one off and sets the last of the six-pack on the other side of the desk in front of two empty chairs.

"Have a seat."

They stand in the doorway, and Father Vaughan looks up as he pops the tab on his Coke can with a satisfying release of pressure. He takes a sip and raises his eyebrows as he drinks, looking again at the cans and the empty chairs. The room is so quiet Mouse can hear the carbonation fizzing in the Priest's mouth before he swallows.

They sit. He smiles.

"What brings you to the House of the Lord at this late hour?" He opens his desk drawer. "Obviously, I can see you didn't come to steal a Game Boy."

They open their Cokes. Only Eddie takes a sip, followed by a belch he is unable to stifle. Mouse is looking at the ceiling.

"Vincent." Father Vaughan says the name with the special authority that only men of the cloth or teachers can employ.

Mouse looks at the Priest, and then to the floor.

He is a career criminal and a damned good thief. This is different. This is the neighborhood.

He has no interest in causing harm to Father Vaughan, and no opportunity for escape. There is only one option.

He reaches into the chest pocket of his coat, and pulls out the knife. He sets it on the desk, still saying nothing, and takes a sip of his Coke.

"Vincent..." the Priest intones, in the calm voice of many penances...

"Father, no disrespect. We'll be on our way. This was the only thing we came for. We're very sorry."

"VERY sorry, Father," adds Eddie. The room is silent as Father Vaughan draws a deep breath and considers it.

"Very well. I'll expect to see you soon, Vincent, where we can discuss this in a more private setting. You know my hours."

Still staring at the floor.

"Yes, Father."

Being caught by a Priest has turned many a grown man back into a ten-year-old Bible student. Vincent would have no chance of redeeming himself with the people he cares about if he hadn't just surrendered it.

Besides: they got in here once. They can do it again later.

"And you, Edward. Consider this a chance to make a fresh start. You're a family man. Your family deserves better decisions on your part, do they not?"

"Yeah." He taps his chest with the top of his fist after another small burp from drinking his Coke too quickly.

Father Vaughan stands and tips the can upside down, drinking the last of his fifth Coke of the day. Sundays are always slightly heavier consumption days for him. He typically tries to keep it down to three on weekends. He usually fails. His teeth testify to this.

"I assume you came through the broken door?"

Both men nod.

"It's being watched more closely now. Follow me."

The back door to the office leads to a spiral stairwell. They follow him down, and he walks to the cellar door at the end of the Children's Hallway that Vincent-Mouse knows very well.

Father Vaughan opens the cellar door and flips on the second of a pair of light switches. A dim light begins to warm up.

"Mind the steps, men. They're old. After you."

Eddie steps first, and Mouse turns at the top step to apologize again. The door, being slammed before he's out of the way, greets him full-on in the face.

Mouse tumbles into Eddie, and the two of them fall the full set of old wooden stairs together, hard. They land on the concrete floor, bruised and surprised.

"Son of a…"

The door reopens, and the lights are turned off. The Priest is at the top of the stairs, silhouetted in the red EXIT lights of the hallway.

"You came for the knife. You obviously know what it can do. The enemies of God face His judgment. Peace be with you."

And the door slams again. They hear it lock.

A deep voice to their immediate left sends a powerful shiver down their spines.

THIS WILL GO MUCH BETTER FOR YOU

IF YOU DO NOT STRUGGLE.

It strikes twice before they can respond, two sharp talons digging deep into their flesh, with a speed that cuts the very air. Neither man is armed. Had they been, there would not have been time to produce a weapon anyway.

Both men are lifted into the air. It feels like their attacker didn't need any effort to snatch them off their feet, as if they were both stuffed with feathers. Vincent is pulled toward it first, long teeth digging into the spot where his neck meets his shoulder. He gurgles as his shoulder blade is shattered and a large chunk of his neck is bitten out under the ear.

That sickening gurgle is the last sound Eddie will hear before he suffers the same wounds.

The men are deposited onto the floor with an unceremonious thud. Their attacker's scaly skin glistens in the sudden light of the open cellar door. It is a dark, forest green.

The creature shivers and expands in the middle as it inhales, struggling to bring up any hint of fire from the spot in its throat where the gland once burned.

Nothing.

No matter. It won't be her first uncooked meal.

The Priest strolls casually down the stairs without turning the light back on. He is carrying a Coca-Cola flashlight. He shines the beam around the room until it meets the beast's tallow-yellow eyes.

"I've known one of these men since his birth.

Christened him into The Church. How did he come to know about the weapon?"

I BELIEVE THE DEVIL HAS COME TO STOP OUR WORK AND HAS BEGUN TO CORRUPT YOUR FLOCK.

Father Vaughan turned off the flashlight, and walked over to the lights. He turned on the softer mercury light switch, which took longer to power up and was kinder to the creature's eyes.

FETCH THE KNIFE. WE DARE NOT WAIT TO DESTROY THE FINGER OF THE DEVIL ANY LONGER.

Father Vaughan looked at the bodies on the floor and wept.

"What good are my visions if they cannot serve to protect you?"

The Beast turned to face the massive furnace.

YOUR VISIONS ARE OF THOSE WHO HAVE COMMITTED GREAT SINS. YOUR TASK IS TO BRING ME THOSE UPON WHOM GOD HAS PASSED JUDGMENT.

The Beast spun around again, to gesture at the still-twitching bodies, rapidly bleeding out.

THESE MEN, AND THE OTHERS WHO HAVE TRESPASSED HERE, HAVE COME TO STOP US.

"And become our enemies by standing against us."

HE THAT IS NOT WITH ME, IS AGAINST ME.

"Matthew 12:30. I understand. I will leave you to your work."

Father Vaughan walked up the stairs, turning

off the mercury light, closing the door behind him.

He spoke softly to himself, as he mounted the stairs.

"And he that gathers not with Me, scatters abroad."

It was completely by chance that The Mayor saw the sliver of light through the small, cloudy cellar window at St. George's. On, then warming slowly, then off. Then on, warming slowly, then off again. By the time the light comes on a third time, The Mayor has pulled Zoey close and is whispering in her ear.

"I'm going in there, Zoey. If I do not come back, you are to walk down to St. Brigid and tell the nurse at the Emergency Desk to call the Police. Okay?"

She looks down the street. There isn't much traffic tonight. "Okay."

"Wait thirty minutes. Wait over there by the bank and use their clock. I will walk over there to find you."

Zoey nods, and The Mayor of Seventeenth Avenue creeps in through the broken front entrance of St. George's Catholic Church.

He moves very slowly and quietly toward the down staircase, his thin shoes wet and squeaking slightly on the floor.

He turns the corner towards the hallway that leads to the cellar door and is surprised to find a man swathed all in black, with a cane at his side, holding a finger up as if to shush him. The man speaks in whispers.

"Even if your shoes hadn't betrayed you, your smell would have, old man. This is a dangerous place tonight. You should find somewhere else to sleep."

He looks hard into The Mayor's eyes, and his face softens.

"I see. You are more than you appear, aren't you? You do not seek shelter. You seek information about what is going on in the cellar."

The Mayor nods.

The man points for them to leave. The Mayor hears Father Vaughan talking in the cellar, saying something in a language he doesn't recognize.

The Mayor holds up a finger, and walks softly to the cellar door. The man in black follows.

As they reach the top of the stairs, The Mayor hears a second voice, a very deep voice that chills the hair on his head and raises a crop of goose pimples up through the dirt and dead skin on his arms.

They leave through the broken door and cross the street. The Mayor whistles and Zoey appears under the huge sign beside the bank. The lights on the sign display the same two messages repeatedly. Fifty-three degrees. 10:18 PM.

He waves at her, and she nods. She turns and disappears into the night.

"You carry the scent of the street, sir," the man begins, as they walk up the street, away from the corner of Church and Seventeenth. "I gather you have lived there for many years."

"And you, if I may, carry the unmistakable scent of serpents. I believe I saw your snakes this morning. There were a lot of them."

"Indeed. They mean no harm. They will go when my work is done."

The man stops walking, and the cats in Adrian's Alley go silent. Chairman Meow watches his old master talk to the man who made him nervous earlier. In his little cat mind, he hopes the old man will sort this person out.

"Your...*work*."

"You also strike me as someone I can confide in. An ally who can help me complete my work."

The Mayor smiles. "I'm flattered. Allow me to introduce myself. I am The Mayor of Seventeenth Avenue. This is my domain. I am ruler of everything from St. Brigid Regional Hospital to beyond the tracks. I have an elaborate network of informants who make sure we have a good life here, creating our homes as we can. We depend on one another."

"And yet, with a vast network at your disposal, you know nothing of the creature in the cellar of the church and did not know I was here."

The Mayor considers this.

"Paper has been ill today."

"I see."

"I admit that I may have missed a few headlines."

The Duck Man steps out of Adrian's Alley and shouts at them in a friendly voice.

"President Jolie visiting Ecuador! Hopes to return with three new children and a nice bundle of kindling to keep warm! Gas reaches a bajillion dollars a gallon in California! Rangers beat the 49ers by five points and a ham sandwich!"

The Mayor smiles. "Which Rangers? New York or Texas?"

The Duck Man shrugs.

"Thank you, Duck Man," The Mayor says, and he gestures down the alley. "Make sure they know about it on Eighteenth."

The Duck Man nods. He grins a horrible smile full of ruined teeth and takes the alley at an awkward jog. Cats scramble to get out of his way. Cats have an exceptional sense of smell. The Duck Man has an exceptional smell.

The man in black considers reminding The Mayor of his real name, his true identity, the life he gave up when the madness overtook him. Perhaps it would be the great awakening the poor old man needs. This does not seem to be the time, though.

"I am called The Bladesman," he says instead. "I am a servant of the Lord Our God, come to vanquish His enemy, who has come to reside in the protection of God's Own House."

The Mayor's stricken mind processes this. He doesn't know this man, and strangers are, by nature, not to be trusted. But something about this man suggests that he is on the level.

"Tell me more, Bladesman."

Across the street, in the shadows beside the huge bookstore called Spines that has just shut its lights for the evening, Paper watches The Mayor talk to someone he doesn't recognize. This is an

188

unusual thing because it is Paper's business to know everyone. He slips around to the darker shadows and struggles to hear what they might be saying. He can't make out anything, but The Mayor seems to be comfortable with the man.

They talk for at least 30 minutes, and then The Mayor walks home to the Pierce Building. The figure in black walks to the basement of the Porter Building at Church Street and descends into her cellars.

Paper follows him, coughing and rubbing his nose.

Through a window, Paper sees him enter into a forgotten storage room with a small barred window and window-well. Paper skulks over there as casually as he can, and peers in.

He draws a breath, sharp enough that he has to run away to cough without being discovered.

The room is full of snakes. Huge snakes, probably a hundred or more of them. The figure in black steps into the middle of them, and the room begins to fill with a kind of purple mist.

As Paper stares at the scene...no longer all that concerned about being spotted...he sees the thin outline of a pair of great and terrible wings spreading out from the man's back. The wings have sharp edges, not particularly birdlike, or insect-like, a unique shape that may or may not actually exist.

The figure spreads these wings out as far as he can and holds his cane out in front of him upright.

The two biggest snakes Paper has ever seen

in his life weave their way up either side of the cane intertwining with each other until they reach the top of the cane and face each other, heads held back.

Paper has seen this symbol before, in tarnished steel high on the front wall of St. Brigid Regional Hospital. He doesn't know the name for it, but he has just witnessed the formation of a living cadeuses.

He runs to the Pierce Building, faster than he has run since the day he lost his hand.

The Bladesman seems to melt into the floor, disappearing into the mass of serpents, gathering his energy for the task that awaits him.

The Priest pulls the knife out of his robe and sets it in the steel box. He is a little surprised to see the creature flinch a bit as he does so. There is the slightest hint of cowering.

YOU BROUGHT THE HOLY WATER?

"Of course. More than enough to cover it."

POUR ALL OF IT IN THE BOX.

Father Vaughan does, and he recites a Latin incantation as he closes the lid. After a moment, the box begins to shake of its own volition. Then it seems to be jumping as if the knife is trying to force the top from the box and escape. And then it is silent.

IT IS FINISHED. WHAT WAS CHARMED, NO LONGER IS.

The Priest tries to get a feel for the item, tries

to see a history. His sight fails him, though, as it always does with the creature. Whatever sorcery or devilry was at work here with the knife must remain known only to the creature.

YOU MAY DESTROY IT NOW.

The door to the incinerator pulls itself open, and the creature disappears into the shadows of the cellar once more.

Father Vaughan throws the box in, grabs a rag to keep from burning his hand on the handle, and closes the door.

It's nearly noon on Tuesday when Pete Gravy's wife Haley walks into the church for Confession. She is a petite, slender young woman. Beautiful, but wearing the sad, unmistakable air of a *victim* about her. She has the kind of face you have trouble shaking an hour later. And she makes a very powerful distraction for the 13 year-old altar boys putting sharpened pencils in the backs of the pews for Father Vaughan. Each of them knows her missing husband. Each of them has eaten at his restaurant, which is now hers. Each of them has taken in her beauty before and wondered how an abusive schmuck like Pete Gravy deserved a gorgeous woman like that.

Father Vaughan steps into the confessional shortly after she does. The hairs stand on his arm when he pulls the window open. What little he can see of her through it is enough.

His Gift takes over, as is its way.

He sees a living room with mismatched, old furniture. A man is drinking beer and watching a game on TV. The Priest can see this woman in the background, even though he has yet to see her face. He sees her step out of the kitchen with a plastic bowl of popcorn and offer it to the man.

He knows it to be her. Her energy is all over the vision, and her face is starting to come into focus. He recognizes her as one of his flock.

The man says something to her that makes her wince, and he flips the bowl up into the air out of her hands. It bounces on the floor, surrounded by the kernels. He snorts, grins, and turns up the game.

The woman walks back through the kitchen door, only to emerge again a few seconds later. She walks up behind his chair with a purpose.

One of the teams just kicked an extra point, and a television time-out is about to begin. In that brief second of black screen before the endless commercials for beer and pizza begin, he can see her reflection.

With all her might, Haley is swinging a frying pan at him…

"Father? Are you there?"

The Priest hears her words, but they are faint, almost dreamlike. The visions have all of his attention.

He sees another man sleeping beside her in a warm bed in a comfortable room. Snow is falling outside the window. Christmas lights twinkle above the window, dangling from the roof that slants over the bedroom.

"Yes, my child. I am sorry."

"Forgive me, Father…"

…the man is lying in his own blood, a shocked look on his face…

"…for I have sinned."

A bright day in the desert. She is driving a convertible, and she is laughing. A young man in a letter jacket is tied up in the trunk, choking on the rag she forced into his mouth.

"It has been two months, well, I guess three months since my last confession."

She is walking away from a fourth man, barely in his twenties by the look of him, hanging from a thick rope in a barn. She is smiling.

"Go on, my child."

He doesn't hear a word she says. Instead, he watches as she repeatedly stabs a man in a very smart three-piece suit with a steak knife. He sees her smother an old man in a hospital bed with a pillow. He watches as she fires a hunting rifle into the skull of a man in hunting camouflage in a thick forest of pines. She seems to be staring right at him while she slashes the throat of a man in a Motley Crue t-shirt in an alley. Two other men die by her hand the same way, again in the same alley. She seems to be looking right at him and smiling.

"Father?"

She has opened the door of the confessional and is looking at him, smiling that same smile. There is a light in her eyes, a fire that both burns his soul and chills him to his very bones.

"I am sorry, Haley. I was…contemplating."

"Are you all right?"

He smiles a reassuring grin. "Walk with me, my child. You can trust me."

Downstairs, the occupant of the cellar opens a large, yellowing eye.

The weight of sin coming toward the stairwell is intoxicating.

Paper is running to The Mayor's boiler room at the Pierce Building. He is also running a high fever and hallucinating a little as he shivers and shakes at the top of the exterior stairwell.

"Mister Mayor!" he cries out. He sits on the top step and leans against the cool steel handrail.

A man with a briefcase has just stepped out of the Pierce building. He turns the corner of the building to light his cigarette out of the wind of Seventeenth Avenue and sees Paper sitting on the top step, facing away from him.

"Mister Mayor!" Paper's voice is weak. He tries to stand, but lands on his backside again on the top step.

"You okay, kid?"

Paper doesn't respond. He falls onto his back at the edge of the sidewalk.

The man starts to dial 911, and then hangs up. He looks up and sees St. Brigid Hospital dominating his view only a block and a half away.

He hails a cab and picks Paper up. His sympathy deepens when he notices the child has only one hand. By now, a small crowd has gathered, but none of The Mayor's subjects are among them. No one is there who would know who Paper is.

The Mayor is actually a few blocks away at St. George's trying to find a way into the cellar. The lock is strong, and even though he has enlisted one of Paper's boys who is a genius with his picks, every click they hear is for naught.

"I *swear* I got it four times already, Mister Mayor."

"I thought so too, lad. It's ok. Try again."

The boy works the metal pins against the tumblers, and they click again. However, when the knob is tried, it again remains firmly locked.

"I'm sorry. I dunno why it ain't goin'. I'll give it another go."

Another 10 seconds work and another click. This time it is a louder one, and the boy and The Mayor look at one another and smile.

The Mayor tries the knob, and once again, it won't turn.

"Weirdest lock ever. Like God doesn't want us to break in or somethin'. Whadda you need in there, anyway?"

"Never mind, Spider. Run along and get back to your work. When your shift ends, stop and see me. I have cookies and milk at the office."

Spider smiles. "Thanks, Mister Mayor!"

The Mayor tries in vain to peer into the tiny, grimy window that stares down at the cellar. It's one of those thick block windows, decorative glass not meant to be seen through.

The Mayor frowns and crosses Church Street, wondering whether he should approach Father

Vaughan or not. In the light of day, the Bladesman's story makes less and less sense.

It is hard to believe that The Priest is serving The Devil and hiding its creature.

The Mayor crosses Seventeenth at Adrian's Alley for a short walk behind First Methodist Church. Under the rock where Paper's people leave him notes, they are piling up.

Where is that boy?

"He's at St. Brigid, Mayor. A Good Samaritan dropped him at the emergency room when his fever overtook him."

The Mayor is startled at the reply to a question he'd only asked himself in his mind.

The Bladesman is sitting on a brick wall on the other side of the alley. He is absent-mindedly twirling his cane with the ease of someone who has walked with it for many years.

"His fever?"

"It is for the best. Tonight is the night, and Paper will be safer there."

The Mayor drops the stone onto the paper scraps without reading them. He does not violate Paper's trust. "So, you are God's Surgeon?"

The Bladesman dropped down from the wall.

"Mayor, the only way to stop the beast is to remove the heart. The only way to remove the heart is with one of the Holy Blades. I cannot destroy her, but I can at least contain her and stop her from gathering more power."

"And you possess one of these Holy Blades?"

"I do. In addition, I caution you to avoid St. George's until this is over. The information I shared with you last night was designed solely to keep you and your people safe."

"I understand." The Mayor looks toward the street. "But do you..."

He looks back over to the wall, but he is alone in the alley.

Tuesday night brings another thunderstorm, but the heaviest rain is brief and followed by a light but steady shower.

A huge pile of snakes separate from each other, and the Bladesman rises up from the center of them. They return to their complex knots as soon as he steps away from them.

What happens next for them is unspoken, understood. If the Bladesman returns, and he is wounded...they are to conceal and repair him before his journey home. If he doesn't return by dawn, they will disappear into the nearby hills, a pair at a time, until there is no trace of their time here, except for a lack of mice in the building's basement.

At 9:53, according to Zoe's post-it note, a figure in black slipped into St. George's Catholic Church. Immediately, he smells The Mayor of Seventeenth Avenue. It appears The Mayor has ignored the Bladesman's suggestion to avoid the church, and has been waiting in the shadows.

"Father Vaughan is still here, somewhere. The light is still on in his office. Perhaps we can reason with him. He may not understand -- "

"You are trespassing here, gentlemen. Mister Mayor? You know better than to come in without letting me know you are here. There are insurance questions, you know."

Father Vaughan is descending the stairwell.

"And who have you brought with you?"

The Bladesman removes his cloak and hangs it on a hook in the entryway.

"Father, I am called by many names."

There is a rush of wind and a blinding flurry of lights. Without taking a single step, the Bladesman is suddenly standing on the stairs beside the Priest.

"Look into my eyes and give me my name."

Father Vaughan squints and looks away.

"Search your heart and use your gift, Father Vaughan. Some have called me Vassal of The God of Abraham. Others call me the Punisher of Idolatry, the Restraint Upon The Leviathan, the Surgeon of Order."

The Priest sinks to his knees, shaking.

Finally, he says "Jehoel?"

Yahoel smiles at hearing a version of his name and puts a hand on his head. The Priest has done his homework.

And I have come to set you free.

His voice is different now, and it echoes in the church. It causes The Mayor and The Priest to fall to their knees. The Priest weeps with joy. The Mayor squints at the brilliant light that flows out from the Angel.

With a loud crack, the entire church shakes. A howl rises from the depths of the cellar that grays the hairs on their necks.

DO NOT LISTEN TO THE LIES OF THE DEVIL!

Father Vaughan, still on his knees and filled with nervous spasms, looks up at Yahoel.

The touch of the Angel has lifted a veil, and with his gift, he can see a history as old as the world of men. Of wars fought between walled cities. Societies punished by God as plagues ripped through the unjust and those who would protect the name of their God took up flaming swords.

He sees the late wielder of the charmed knife he so recently corrupted for what and who he truly was. The vision fills him with regret.

As Father Vaughan stares into nothingness, seeing much, The Mayor of Seventeenth Avenue stands back up.

The Mayor looks into Yahoel's eyes, and for the briefest of moments, thinks about his mother.

It's the first thought about his true self he's managed to have in a very long time. He can see her face, but he does not remember her name.

Paper wakes up in a hospital bed roughly five minutes after Dr. Bradley Vincent made a few notations on his chart.

His room is dark, but he is aware of a figure dressed all in blue sitting in the chair in the corner of the room. He's not only dressed in blue: He seems to radiate a soft, comforting blue glow.

Jeffrey. His voice echoes in the room, bold and deep.

Paper's hand starts to pull the sheet up to his chin and then stops. He is only frightened for an instant before a strange calm flows over him, and he pushes himself up on his elbows to look in the man's direction.

"Who are you?"

You have been sick, Jeffrey. And you have something important to do tonight. So I am here to make you better. I am called Raphael. His voice is impossibly loud, but it attracts no response from the nurses or anyone else on the staff. They would *have* to be able to hear the man speaking. *This is obviously a dream*, he thinks to himself.

"Are you a doctor?"

Of a sort. The man rises from the chair and slides across the floor to him, without taking a step. Paper notices that the room is impossibly quiet, and no noise is coming from the hallway. Yes, this has to be a dream.

The figure lays a hand upon Paper's sweaty brow. In a blink, Paper feels his mind sharpen, his chest and sinuses clear, and his strength rush back into muscles that no longer ache. Various parts of his body tingle and vibrate in a strange way he has never felt before.

Your friend is at St. George's Church, and he needs you to do something for him.

Instructions are whispered into his ear, and Paper nods in the dim blue light that emanates from the man. As the figure retreats, vanishing into a corner of the shadowy room, Paper notices the return of the normal hospital background noises. His ears are filled with the series of beeps and clicks that tell the staff he is still alive.

It isn't until he jumps out of the bed to dress himself that he notices something incredible.

THIS IS MY TIME, SERAPHIM. THIS IS THE END OF THE WORLD.

The creature is pacing in the darkness below.

YOU CANNOT RESTRAIN THAT WHICH IS CALLED UPON BY THE WORLD ITSELF.

Two men and an Angel stand at the top of the cellar stairwell, listening to the creature's angry pouting.

I have heard no trumpets.

IF IT IS NOT MY TIME, HOW DID I COME TO BE HERE? HOW DID I TAKE THE PRIEST'S GIFT AND BEGIN TO FEED WHILE BRINGING PUNISHMENT TO THE WICKED OF THIS WORLD?

You have not been called upon to perform this duty. This is not your time. The Behemoth is prisoner, and you will not sire the end of the world with him. There is no strength that you can create within yourself to change this. It is Fact.

The stairs are suddenly ripped out from under them with a vicious lashing-out of a long, thick tail. The Mayor and Father Vaughan come crashing down hard amidst the debris.

The Mayor is pinned under part of the handrail. The Priest is badly injured.

201

The darkly dressed Angel, who failed in his attempts to grab them, hovers where the top step had been.

YOU ARE TOO SLOW TO SAVE AN INNOCENT AND A MAN OF THE CLOTH WHO BEARS A SPECIAL GIFT FROM GOD? PERHAPS I HAVE GROWN STRONG ENOUGH TO SOW THE SEEDS OF ARMAGEDDON AFTER ALL.

Yahoel rips the handle from his cane revealing a silver blade. He drops down quickly to the Leviathan, and attacks.

Instinctively, the creature parries, but in the course of knocking the Angel into the outside cellar door, the blade opens a deep gash in her arm. She summons all of her strength and prepares for his next move.

The Angel has not moved yet.

YOU HAVE BEEN HERE FOR SEVEN DAYS, AND THIS WAS YOUR BEST ATTEMPT?

Yahoel rights himself at the crushed door. He reaches for his weapon and discovers the handle has separated from the blade. His weapon has been destroyed. The two pieces of the blade are losing their inner light.

Seven days?

I HAVE BEEN WAITING FOR YOU TO SHOW YOURSELF. SENDING AN UNDERLING IN YOUR STEAD WITH THE GOLDEN KNIFE WAS THE INSULTING ACT OF A COWARD. WHAT HOPE DID HE HAVE OF OVERCOMING HIS BRAVADO AND PERFORMING THE DUTY THAT HAS EVADED HIM FOR MILLENNIA?

The Bladesman says nothing.

HAVE YOU AGED BEYOND USE? HAS THE PURPOSE JEHOVAH STATED FOR YOU SO LONG AGO GROWN SO FAR BEYOND YOUR CAPABILITIES? HAS TIME CHANGED YOU SO MUCH?

The Angel walks over to The Mayor and the Priest. They are still alive. He closes his eyes for a moment in thanks. His thoughts search the building for any trace of a second weapon.

The knife is not here. You were able to destroy a Holy Relic in a Catholic Church?

OVER-CONSECRATION. IF I WERE TO DESTROY A HOLY RELIC BY PROFANE MEANS, THE PRIEST WOULD DOUBT MY DIVINITY. YOUR WEAPONS ARE LIVING THINGS WITH THEIR OWN SPIRITS.

Of a type, I suppose. The Angel begins to heal Father Vaughan.

The creature moves over to the shattered blade.

GIVE TOO MUCH WATER TO A NOMAD WHO HAS CROSSED A GREAT DESERT, AND HE WILL DROWN FROM WITHIN.

The creature looks back at him, her body still facing the broken blade beside the ruined door.

GIVE TOO MUCH MEDICINE TO A SICK MAN, AND IT WILL KILL HIM. OVER-BLESS A BLESSED ITEM, AND IT LOSES ALL GODLINESS. IT WAS SIMPLE TO DEDUCE, RESTRAINER.

The Angel moves the wood pinning The Mayor. He enters his mind and leaves a simple message: *Stay.*

I BELIEVE I WILL TRY THE MORE TRADITIONAL APPROACH WITH THE SILVER BLADE NOW THAT THE PRIEST KNOWS THE TRUTH.

She squats over the pieces of the weapon and urinates on them. The dim bits of light that had shone from the pieces a moment before are gone.

HE POISONED THE SPIRIT WITHIN THE GOLDEN WEAPON FOR ME. HE LAID UPON IT THE BURDEN OF TOO MANY BLESSINGS. THE PRIEST WAS VERY HELPFUL. IS HE DEAD?

No. So you have destroyed two weapons. And yet, I sense another.

The Leviathan stops, still facing the wall.

Do you not sense it as well?

As the Leviathan turns, she sees a young man. He is little more than a boy, really. The boy is jumping from the doorway above the Angel. He grasps a brass letter opener in his two good hands, and a fire burns in his innocent young eyes.

Paper crashes violently into the Leviathan's chest and plunges the blade into her heart three times. As the Leviathan collides into the same cracked door that leads to the outside, Paper finds himself thrown into the pile of ruined lumber that had been the cellar stairwell.

Yahoel walks over to the gasping creature. She is becoming smaller, more human-shaped, as the life pours from her wounds. The letter opener is still in her chest.

I only have been here for two days. The other weapon was found by the Priest many years ago, in a small shop in Rome. He did not know the origin of it any more than the merchant who sold it as a harmless opener of correspondence.

He smiles, tapping the tip of the brass handle very lightly. It is still enough movement to cause her to wince in pain.

This is not your time either, Leviathan. I restrain you in the name of Almighty God.

He plunges the letter opener deeper still with a sudden push on the end of the handle.

The Leviathan takes in a hard breath. She then writhes and goes limp.

Before their eyes, she fades into nothingness, leaving no trace beyond a thin film of dust on the cellar floor.

The letter opener clatters to the floor.

The Angel Yahoel fills the cellar with a stark white light, and The Mayor and Father Vaughan feel the last of their aches and pains from the battle disappear entirely. Paper squints and runs for the unhinged, crushed outer door.

He looks up into the sky, and as much as is possible in the thick of the city…he sees stars for the first time in far too many nights. The clouds are gone.

The Mayor of Seventeenth Avenue is thinking. Thinking about the strange entry he has just made in the official Record. Thinking about never speaking about it all again.

Thinking about a nice car he remembers. A

silver one from Bavaria. Whose car was that?

He sits with his back to the wall of the Pierce Building. The wall is cool this time of the morning, even through his coat. Soon it will be 88 degrees, and the wall will not feel this good. He is happy to be leaning against it now, rather than later.

Kitty-corner across the street, the fair maiden in the green leotard is walking up to the entrance of Contours. For some reason, he can picture her in the Bavarian car quite clearly.

Paper walks up from Grove Street and takes a seat at The Mayor's right. With both hands, he fumbles through the notes that have been left for him behind the Methodist Church.

"A busy couple of days."

The Mayor says nothing but nods.

"Still no sign of Mouse and Eddie. I guess they…"

Paper doesn't finish his thought.

"Did you see where he went after he…?"

The Mayor puts a finger to Paper's lips, still staring across the corner.

Two snakes slither past them, headed to the arbor at the corner of Grove Street and Fourteenth Avenue. One of them will be run over by a passing car, right itself, and continue, flattened.

Paper runs his fingers through his greasy hair.

All 10 of them.

The city is waking up. It's going to be a beautiful day today.

Epilogue

One Friday morning after talking to Zoey, who has back-to-school shopping to do today, Paper is cracking his knuckles. It's something he had always wanted to do and couldn't. Now he can't seem to stop doing it. He smiles every time he does it. *Every* time.

Paper watches a man in a football jersey place his hoagie and soft drink cup on the top of the busted newspaper box.

He has a cell phone wedged between his head and his right shoulder. Paper knows this to be the classic sign of someone who isn't going to manage to close the door completely, and that he can get his daily copy of the Times-Dispatch.

"Yeah, bush-league call all the way," the man in the jersey says to his phone. "The league's gotta start crackin' down on these refs. Cost us the game."

He pops some change into one of the slots on the little metal box and pulls the handle. He takes out a newspaper and releases the door.

"You ain't kiddin," he says.

He folds the paper and tucks it into his right

armpit as he picks up his sandwich from Pete's and his coke. He walks away from the newspaper box, continuing a fascinating discussion that calls into question the intelligence, lineage, and even the sexual orientation of the referees in professional football. His friend on the other end of the call is doing the same.

Paper walks up to the box and gently pulls.

He reaches in and pulls out a single copy of the Thursday morning edition. He lets the door go and presses the handle in a bit before trying it a second time. It is locked.

He smiles, satisfied that no one else can take advantage of the generosity of the old box, and turns.

He freezes.

A man is smiling at him from the driver's seat of a blue Taurus. He has both hands resting on the window ledge of the door, and obviously has been staring directly at Paper the entire time.

"Hey kid…come here for a second, willya?"

The logo stickered onto the door is that of the Times-Dispatch with the words Circulation Department underneath it.

The man smiles again.

Paper weighs his options in a split second. Running is not one of them. Running has never historically accomplished anything positive in his life. Especially here on Seventeenth Avenue.

He frowns, shrugs, and walks over to the car.

In the rear-view mirror, the man sees a spot open up right behind him on the street, and he holds a finger up at Paper as he backs the car up, parks it in the spot, and locks it.

Paper waits. He isn't sure why he waits, but he does.

As the man walks up to him, Paper's first instinct is to hold out the newspaper. The man holds a hand up and shakes it at him, dismissing the offer.

"Keep it. I've been watching you do this on and off for about a month now. I just wanted to talk to you. Have you had breakfast yet?"

Paper shakes his head. "Nope."

The man points toward the hospital. "How about the Skillet? Great omelets there."

"Sure are," Paper says, and they begin to walk towards Market Plaza. It is only a few blocks away and the sun has made it a very pleasant morning today finally trying to dry everything out from the recent rain.

"So, every day you take one newspaper from the box. Only one. It's a bad box I've never managed to replace, and you take advantage of it pretty much every day...except a couple of days last week.

"I was sick. I was even in the hospital with it."

"Oh. Hoping you're feeling better now."

"I am, thanks."

"I thought you were also...um..." He abandons the comment. There is no delicate way to say 'disfigured'.

"Anyway," he says, "who do you get the newspapers for?"

"They're for me," Paper says flatly. "It's my

209

job to know what's going on. The Times does a great job covering the news."

"Well, thank you. We do try."

They walk on, passing the Pierce Building.

"You really read each and every issue of my newspaper?"

"Each and every issue, yes. Usually twice."

"You're an unusual young man then. Most kids won't touch a newspaper unless their parents are making them clean out the birdcage or housetrain a puppy or they've ordered the fish at the Irish place."

"I like to know what's going on," Paper says. "Here and everywhere."

"I like that too."

Paper takes a chance. "So, how much trouble am I in, Mr. Harmon? Your name is Sheldon Harmon, right? I see you listed in the front of the paper every day as the Circulation Manager. I can't imagine the Times-Dispatch would give anyone else a vehicle with the Circulation Department written on it. Newspapers don't make the kind of money they did in the old days."

Sheldon is surprised but continues walking. "My personal car, actually. I get a small stipend for having it logoed up. Makes the gas a little more affordable. You have me at a disadvantage, kid. I don't know *your* name."

"People call me Paper."

Sheldon smiles and turns down the little sidewalk facing Piedmont Street that contains the front door to Skillet. "I was hoping that was who you are. I've heard of you."

"You have?"

"Two, please," he says to the young lady who greets them at the door. She is wearing a brown apron, a ponytail, a nametag that reads JEANETTE, and a smile. She hopes there will be a nice tip. There will be.

They sit at a booth, and Jeanette puts a pair of large laminated menus in front of them, she fills two water glasses from a pitcher, and promises to be back in a minute.

"Everyone in this part of the city knows who Paper is. You collect information. You keep an eye on things. You're a very important cog in the machine that keeps the guy they call The Mayor in power. It shouldn't work, but it does. I had also heard that you were missing a hand, but that doesn't seem to be the case."

Paper dismisses the last part of it and smiles. "We take care of our own here on Seventeenth. We get the job done."

"I like that you do what you do, Paper, and I admire the way you do it. Even if it includes you stealing a newspaper from me every day."

"Yeah, about that..."

Sheldon smiles and shakes his head. "We're putting a new machine in there next week. It will be harder for you to get your news that way."

Paper nods and purses his lips. "Yeah, I guess it will."

"So, come work for me."

Paper shoots the man a look. "Come work for you?"

"Are we ready to order?"

"Not yet, Jeanette. Give us just one more minute, if you would."

"Certainly," she says, as bubbly as one can without being horribly fake about their enthusiasm.

"It just so happens that my regular paperboy for the residential route of Seventeenth from Piedmont out to Copperline Street decided to quit yesterday. How old are you?"

"Old enough."

Sheldon Harmon smiles. "We can sort that out later. Are you in? You'll have to get up early, but you get a free newspaper out of it and a chance to learn a little about the business."

Copperline, Paper thinks to himself. *I guess I'm due to finally start crossing the tracks now anyway.*

Jeanette comes back. Before she can say anything, Paper looks up and says "Denver omelet, links not patties, and apple juice, please."

He looks across the booth.

"What do you want, boss?"

Sheldon smiles again. "That sounds good to me. I'll have the same."

A conversation...

"IT IS DIFFICULT TO SEE YOU."

"s'Only a little fog," the shabby little man replied. He spread his arms and breathed in deep, his chest inflating like an air mattress. The fogs in the city always smelled nice to him. Perhaps it was the trees at the lower reaches of the adjacent mountain range. Many of them could be found on Seventeenth. A few were even planted around St. George's Church.

The Creature drew itself up to impressive size and took a breath. "I TRUST THAT YOU - "

"Have you seen the trees?" The Mayor interrupted. "I mean...on a day unlike this, when the air is clear and you can see past the West Side? We have a beautiful ring of trees around the mountain. Pines and Firs. Beeches and Birches."

The creature did not reply. So much as it was possible for it to wear a confused look, it did so.

The Mayor of Seventeenth Avenue continued.

"These are trees that shouldn't grow together. In nature, they compete for the soil. The root system of one species always wins out and gets rid of the others. Similar to how the English tried to breed out the Scots. *Prima Nocta*, they called it. The nobleman's seed beats the husband's seed to the punch because the wealthy landowner gets the first night with the new bride, and - "

"ENOUGH."

"...it was in a movie or something. I think I remember seeing Longshanks saying something about..."

"I AM NOT INTERESTED IN ANY OF THIS."

"What are you interested in? Why are you here? Were you summoned, somehow?"

"I HAVE ALWAYS BEEN HERE. I HAVE BEEN IN THE HEARTS OF ALL OF YOU, LITTLE MAN. ALWAYS."

The Mayor struggled for the appropriate response to this. None came.

"YOU MEN HAVE ALWAYS SOUGHT TO ELIMINATE ONE ANOTHER. YOU CLAW FOR YOUR OWN SUCCESS AT THE EXPENSE OF THOSE AROUND YOU. I AM YOUR NATURE MADE FLESH. I AM HUNGER. I AM POWER. I AM FORCE."

The Mayor turned around and looked in the direction of the mountains. They were just beginning to emerge from the fog.

"You are totally missing the point about the trees."

The creature wheezed. The sound developed until it had rolled into hearty laughter. The laugh made The Mayor shiver a bit, like stepping out of a hot shower into a heavily air-conditioned room.

The shabby man tried not to show this as he waited for the grotesque monster to stop mocking him.

"YOUR TREES DO NOT INTEREST ME."

"The trees." The Mayor sighed. He looked toward them, and they continued to become more visible as the sun rose and burned away the fog.

"THE TREES."

"The trees. They work *together*. They really shouldn't, but they do. No one's sure why. They pull from the same soil and twirl all of their roots together."

"I HAVE SEEN TREES OF A DIFFERENT SORT GROW TOGETHER BEFORE."

"Here, they make each other stronger. At the foot of the mountain, they grow together underground, sharing the thin layer of soil. They prop one another up in the face of wind, and mudslides, and the occasional man-made disaster."

"YOU ARE QUITE ELOQUENT FOR AN UNCLEAN MAN WITHOUT A HOME."

"I have a home. This city is my home. This strip of blacktop is my home. And all these people..."

He gestured with his arm, sweeping it to the northeast up Seventeenth.

"...they are my family. There is nothing I wouldn't do for them."

"TREES IN A FOREST."

"Trees in a forest, yes."

The creature was silent for a moment. It shuffled in the dim sunlight as it broke through the trees of Grove Park. The light came into the park at the exact spot where Darius Prince had died. It made The Mayor smile to think that the grandson of The Proud Prince would carry the light into the park for eternity. A chance at last for the boy to shine.

"Even in death," The Mayor mumbled, his face painted in sorrow, "you fail to understand us."

"DEAD."

The Mayor smiled. "Yes, dead. Have you forgotten?"

"HOW…"

"You're only around in my dreams now. You're just a memory."

"PERHAPS I AM MORE, HUMAN. I AM ANGER. I AM HUNGER. I AM ETERNAL. I AM NEVER TRULY GONE.

"Perhaps," The Mayor said. "But I will wake up soon. I will still hold sway over Seventeenth Avenue. I will breathe this glorious air."

He turned to look at the creature. It was hard to make out the form of the beast, but the fog was completely gone now. The Leviathan had begun to fade, a ghost without shadows in which to hide.

"And you will not."

Acknowledgements

Before anything else, I should thank Hannah Monroe, Leslie Diehl, and my daughter Emily Williams. They posed for the cover of the last novel, *Mulligan's Daughters*, and didn't get a proper thank-you in the acknowledgements.

Thanks also to Hollie Ayers, who edits everything I write and has forgotten more about grammar than I will ever remember.

This story is for everyone who read *For Four Players* and said, "The Mayor was my favorite story in the book," or "The Mayor was good but it should have been longer." Which was pretty much each of you that bought *For Four Players* from me.

This story was intended to be a novel when I first starting messing with it. At the time it was called *Paper*. When the first two attempts to write it ended in frustration, I thought it might work better as a short story and put it aside for a few years. I threw it together somewhat quickly when I did the book of short stories.

The more I played around with it, though, the more I had other ideas about how to make it a novel again. When I was trying to decide what book to work on in the fall of 2012…it seemed like the one to go with.

I still feel like there might be a little more to this story, but I felt the book was done when I wrapped it up. I might revisit Seventeenth at some point.

The Beloved Kim has become my (possibly unwilling) story collaborator for all of my recent novels. She reads with great passion, and provides me the very best nudges when I suffer from writer's block. She also took the cover photo for this book again because I have no talent at all with a camera. Having a wife so willing to put up with how obsessive I become when I write is so much more than I deserve.

All hail the Golumpki Queen of Parma, Ohio. She knows who she is. Any time a talented artist takes an interest in someone else's creativity, the vibe is just what you need to keep going when you find yourself depleted of energy. Thank you, Beth.

Furthermore, my thanks to the South Bend NaNo group, and I hope they had as much fun on their own projects as I did on mine.

This book is also a signpost for my nephew, Corey Ayres. You, my Apple, are going to write stories far better than this one someday, and I can't wait to have you sign them all for me.

And thank you to my son, Skylar. For a month, when he came to visit on the weekend, I spent too much time buried in a laptop.

This book is dedicated with brotherly love to Reverend Ryno. I miss you, Ryan. It totally sucks that you aren't here to read this one. You really liked the story when we talked about it.

From a fresh Keep On The Borderlands,
November 2012

About the author

At the time this book was written, Tommie Lee was the Production Manager at WSBT Radio as well as the "Memorex Nightfly" at 99.9 WHFB-FM in South Bend. A lot of it was written in the space of three weeks during his lunch breaks in their opulent break room, which most of the employees do not use.

Tommie was formerly the co-host of *Tommie & The Bartender* morning show on *95.3 WAOR*. It was a Classic Rock radio station that was murdered in a far more fiendish way than any of the characters in his horror novel *Chair de ma Chair*. Tommie has worked in radio since Halloween, 1988. It was a bad decision, sure, but he was very young when he made it.

Before that, he thought he was a musician. It turned out he wasn't. Previous to that, he was writing fiction in his bedroom on his mother's old typewriter and a C64. Now, he is married with two teenagers, a cat, and a dog. They all tolerate his occasional bouts of incessant typing.

This is his fourth novel.

Connect with the author

You can find Tommie online at *tkcbooks.com*, which also has links to his narcissistic ramblings on Twitter and Facebook.

He welcomes your feedback emails about the story at tlc@tealsea.com. He writes back. He's on Twitter as @tlcjr and talks about his books under @AuthorTLee.

If you liked this book, tell people by posting a review of it somewhere. Every time he notices that someone has bought one of his books, he does a disturbing little "Sales Dance" that freaks out his dog, Duchess. He enjoys freaking Duchie out whenever possible...

http://www.tkcbooks.com
http://www.facebook.com/tkcbooks

Made in the USA
Charleston, SC
23 June 2013